I'd Rather BE YA HITTA

Finding Love in Little Havana

A NOVEL BY

PORSCHEA JADE

PROLOGUE

Rebekah.

"Mikalson! Up front. You have a visitor!"

Hearing my name being called caused me to jump up out of my bunk and try to make out as much as I could through the little opening in the door. I had been locked up for three months since my boyfriend died without so much as a peep from anyone. No answered phone calls, no visitations, not even a peep from my lawyer; but now on today of all days, someone wants to grace me with their presence.

"Who is it?" I asked the guard once he approached my door.

"Do you want the visitation or not, Fish? I don't have all day."

"Um. Yeah. Just give me a moment to freshen up," I told him.

"You have five."

Scurrying around my cell, I threw on my pants and tried to make myself as presentable as possible. I'm not sure who was on the other side of the door, but I was willing to find out if it meant that it got me out of solitary confinement.

"Ready or not, Fish, I'm comin' in," the guard said.

Standing up straight, I stood in the door, still waiting for him to come in and escort me to my visitation. I knew the routine: pat me down to make sure I wasn't taking anything out; unlock my wrist from the chain that kept me confined there; and then, make sure that my T-shaped chains were secured.

Making my way down the dimly lit hallway, I followed the guard as I tried to take in my surroundings. Trying to keep mental notes of everything I saw, I noticed that we were going in the opposite direction than where the signs were pointing for the visitation room.

"Weren't we supposed to take that left back there? I thought you said I had a visitor?" I asked, pointing over my shoulder.

"Shut up and keep walking."

Feeling my heart beat out of my chest, I started to panic as a million and one scenarios played in my mind. Where the hell was he taking me?

Approaching the tall steel door, the guard faced my direction and started to undo my chains and handcuffs. Rubbing my wrists to ease the soreness, I looked onto the Latino guard's face for answers, only to have him divert his eyes from mine.

"This is as far as I go. Go ahead inside. I will be here when you finish," he told me, holding the door open.

My mouth had suddenly become dry as I took tiny footsteps into the brightly lit room. There was a table in the middle of the floor and three well-dressed men that I had never seen before. Two of them stood behind the chair of the man that was sitting in a very protective stance, piquing my interest, and had my mind wondering who this mystery man was.

Sitting down in the empty seat, I brought my eyes up to look at the man that was sitting in front of me. I couldn't make out his facial features because the hat he wore on his head blocked most of his face. The only thing I could make out was his lips and chin.

"You're just as beautiful as Jaiyce claimed you to be, Ms. Rebekah," he said in a very husky voice.

"How do you know Jaiyce?"

"Sweetheart, I know everyone. Jaiyce spoke very highly of you, and to know that you are the one that killed him is very troubling, seeing how much he loved you."

"I didn't kill him! I'll tell you like I told the rest of them. He was already dead when I got home," I told him with aggravation in my voice.

"The courts believe that you're guilty."

"Well the courts are fucking idiots. And so are you if you believe them."

"Watch your tone. If I believed you were guilty, we wouldn't be having this conversation. I would have had someone kill you before you even stepped foot in this prison, and you can bet your life on that," he threatened, sitting up in his seat and taking his hat off.

Taking in his features, tears welled up in my eyes. His emerald colored eyes bore into mine, and I swear I was looking at Jaiyce twenty years into the future.

"Who are you?"

"I think you already know the answer to that," he told me, giving me a slight smile.

"He told me that you were dead."

"Oh, to the world I am. But that's neither here nor there. I have something that I need from you, but first, I need to get you out of here," he said as if it were so simple.

"I'm never getting out of here. I have twenty-five to life," I explained, putting my head down. The thought alone caused tears to fall down my face. I was in jail for a crime I didn't commit, and the one man that I loved more than life was dead. I had no family; all I had was Jaiyce, and now he was gone.

"I can give you two options: Either you can stay in here and live out your life sentence, or you can leave here with me and help me find the people that killed my son. The choice is yours, but I need you to make it in the next thirty seconds.

Lifting my head, I looked at his face to gauge his reaction. I could tell that he was serious. Without thinking twice, I nodded my head. I would search the ends of the Earth to find the people responsible for my pain.

"Once you walk out these doors, Rebekah Mikalson is dead and she can never return. You will live out the rest of your life as a fugitive. There is no turning back after this."

"No one said anything about turning back," I told him, standing to my feet.

That day changed my life forever, and that is how I became one of the most feared and ruthless queen pins that America had ever seen. Walking out of the jail, Rebekah died, but Empriss was born.

CHAPTER ONE

Empriss

Six years later...

Crossing my heels, I kept my eyes trained on the man sitting across from me, while my chrome desert eagle rested on my lap. The room was dimly lit and the only light in the room was the spot light that he sat under.

"Who sent you?" I asked in a calm voice keeping my face out of the light.

"N...no one sent me." He stuttered through busted lips, squirming in the chair that he was bound to.

"Jeffrey, is it? Well see, Jeffrey, the thing is I hate liars, and you called me by a name that I haven't heard in over six years. My name is not Rebekah. She died a very long time ago. The name is Empriss. Now, for you to call me that name means that someone either sent you to find me or... you're lying," I stated, cocking the hammer back and leaning forward in my seat so that he could see my face for the first time.

I kept the mentality of the Grimm Reaper. If you saw my face, you were as good as dead. No one other than the people that I kept in my inner circle saw me and could live to tell about it, but even they would die before they left my camp. No face, no case.

"Empriss, I swear no one sent me. It was a slip of words. I have a daughter and a family to feed. I didn't mean it," he pleaded.

"I hate to repeat myself and you will learn that the hard way. I will only ask you one last time who sent you for me, but please believe, with or without your help, I will find them. The only reason I'm giving you the opportunity to say it yourself is because you should think about your wife and daughter's future.

Either you want them to be financially set for the rest of their lives, or they can struggle with nothing. But the only common thing in those two scenarios are you won't be present. So, you choose," I told him, getting up and walking behind his chair to rest my hand on his shoulders.

He was silently crying, but he nodded his head as the gravity of my words started to weigh on his brain. Slowly massaging his shoulder, I tried to give him his moment because I knew that knowing you were about to die couldn't be easy, but my patience was wearing thin and all I wanted to do was get the name and go on about my way.

The day I escaped from prison, I left with vengeance in my heart. I spent the first two years following every lead that had Jaiyce's name attached to it and left more bodies in my wake than Jack the Ripper, but the fact remained that each lead I followed turned into a new lead and another after that. So once I finally came across the final one, I wasn't ready to face it yet.

I had to become someone else to destroy the people that stole everything from me. I had to be someone other than Rebekah, so I had to let go of her and become the heartless hardened bitch that walked this Earth today. Rebekah was dead and gone, but Empriss roamed the underground in her place.

"His name is Khalid," he finally answered, defeated.

"I'll make sure that your family never wants for nothing, and as much as I appreciate you sharing what you know with me, I can't let you live," I whispered in his ear, sliding the blade I kept in my mouth across his neck.

"Clean this up and find out who the hell this Khalid person is. I'm about to be late for my son's soccer game," I demanded, walking around the chair and out the door without so much as a second glance.

* * * *

"Gooooo, JJ!" I yelled, jumping up to my feet as my baby kicked the soccer ball up the field before kicking it in to the goal. Cheering, I had a smile planted on my face. My son was my world and everything I did, I did it for him. It was rare that I could make it to his games, but when I did, I went all out for him.

Dressed down in a teal sundress, some light brown gladiator sandals, and a light brown fedora to match, I sat in the bleachers without a care in the world like I hadn't just taken a man's life an hour prior. That was Empriss the boss. This was Empriss the mom and caretaker. I enjoyed the times where it was just me and him and I didn't have to focus on anything other than being a carefree parent.

Feeling someone slide next to me, I inhaled a deep breath and tried to keep my attitude in check.

"Not today, Papa. You know this time is off limits."

"If it could wait, you know I wouldn't have interfered," he spoke in his heavy Cuban accent.

Pulling my Chanel frames off my face, I folded them and looked over in his piercing emerald eyes. The same ones that adorned my son's face. The same ones that my ex had.

"What is it, Papa?" I finally surrendered, defeated.

"There is someone requesting your presence in Memphis. A young man by the name of Hamin. He wants a counsel."

"Okay, and what does that have to do with me? You know just as well as I know that I can't stay in the States for long."

"Sometimes, mija, you have to make sacrifices when the situation is beneficial to you," he explained, keeping his eyes on JJ as he continued to play.

"And what benefit is that?" I questioned, raising my eyebrow at him.

"You would have to make the trip to find that out."

Thinking about what he was implying, I started to choke up a little bit. I wasn't scared of many things in my life, but whenever I had to make trips to the States, I got clammy. I've only traveled back to the United States a handful of times since I fled six years ago. Each time, it was to either follow a lead on my deceased ex, or it was to meet a potential distro.

I supplied mainly everything moving in and out of the lower states. If I wasn't the main supplier, then nine times out of ten, their supplier got it from me. Either way it went, I was making money. At the age of twenty-six, I was the youngest queen pin this side of the country had ever seen, but the only difference was I was most feared because no one knew who I was.

"Papa, I don't think I can make this trip."

"You can, and you will. The arrangements have already been made. You leave Friday," he stated just as the coach blew the whistle to announce the end of game.

"Mommy! Did you see me?" JJ yelled, running over to where we sat on the sidelines.

"Yes, baby, I did. I'm so proud of you," I told him standing up and hugging him.

"Did you see me, Papa?"

"Of course. I can't stay, but you and your mother will join me for family dinner tonight, won't you?" Javier asked looking between us.

"Mommy, are we?"

"Yes," I surrendered, looking down into his excited eyes. "Now, go over to say bye to your friends while I finish talking to Papa.

"Yes, ma'am. See you later, Papa." And with that, he ran away to do as he was told.

"What time do I leave?"

"You have a private jet, so the time is up to you, but you need to be at your meeting by 8 p.m. I should go, but I will see you tonight. We can talk more then."

"Okay, Papa," I said, kissing him on his cheek before he walked away just as quickly and quietly as he came.

Friday was three days away, and even though I didn't want to make this long ass trip to Memphis, I knew Javier wasn't asking me. Over the past six years, he had become the father that I never had, and I never wanted to disappoint him. I knew I would be spending the next couple days preparing for my trip, so I would make the most of tonight with my son because there was no telling when I would have another one of these carefree days.

CHAPTER TWO

Hamin

*B*oss was the one word that could describe a nigga like me. At the age of twenty-eight, I had done more in my lifetime than most, but that didn't stop that hunger from growing inside of me. I always heard the old heads say that it was a dog-eat-dog world and niggas was always hungry, and that shit was even more true in the hood.

You never knew what you were gon' get. You could be on top of the world one day, and on ya ass the next. You had ya so-called niggas plotting on you, the feds watching you, and every bitch in a 100-mile radius trying to trap you. The shit was just a gamble, and truth be told, I loved every second of it.

I was never the type to be the prey, I was always the predator. The one meant to be on top. That's why this meeting was so important for me. This plug was like a fucking ghost. No one spoke the name. No one ever saw the face unless you were in the inner circle. All anyone knew for sure was this motherfucka had some of the purest uncut cocaine to ever touch the streets of Memphis, and I was trying to get a piece of the pie.

Double parking my Rover in front of Lamar Terrace, I hit my locks and swaggered in the building without a care in the world. Lamar was ranked one of the most notorious projects in Memphis at one point for its break-ins and drug traffic. Even with knowing that, I moved around as if I owned the place.

Taking the stairs two at a time, I made my way up to the third floor and to the apartment I was looking for. Opening the door without knocking, I stepped in and scanned the room until my eyes landed on who I was looking for.

In the cloud of weed smoke and music was my right-hand man and long-time friend, Ace. Ace had been my boy since we were jits, running around breaking shit, causing as much hell as possible. Walking over to where he sat playing cards, I slapped the back of his neck.

"Yo, nigga, what the fuck!" He started spinning around in his seat. "Mane, what you tryin' to do, get shot or some shit?" He laughed, standing up.

"Whatever, nigga, kill the noise. I'on see no money being made," I commented, looking around the room.

"'Cause you only lookin' witcha eyes. Follow me," he replied, throwing his cards down on the table and making his way down the hall.

Following close behind him, he stopped in the front of the second door to our right and pulled out a set of keys. Unlocking it, he pushed it open and stepped to the side for me to go ahead of him. Stepping inside, I waited for him to lock the door behind us and show me what he wanted me to see.

"You always quick to say a nigga ain't on his shit, but what you fail to realize is I'm a boss nigga. I stay on my shit," he gloated, coming out the closet with four duffle bags then going back inside only to return with two more.

"This yo' count for this month?" I questioned, unzipping one of the bags to see the nicely rolled bundles of bills.

"Along wit' everyone else's. You said you needed this for tonight, right?" he asked, referring to the meeting.

"Yeah. This along wit' the money I got put up should be enough to get us started. I'on know who this cat is, but we need this shit. We ain't nickel and dimin' no more, but I ain't even tryin' to be seen in the streets at all," I explained.

"I feel ya. You already know how I give it up. I bleed this street shit so I'm always down to make more money."

"I hear you," I told him.

See, Ace loved the streets. He was raised in the bottom so that's all he knew. He was okay with where we were in the game, as long as we were making money; and that was good for him, but I ain't see it like that. I wasn't trying to hustle for the rest of my life. I was on some different shit. All I was trying to do was stack my money for the next two years, moving these keys, then I was getting out. A nigga wasn't trying to be no thirty-year old dope boy. That shit was played out.

"Help me get this shit in the truck tho'. I need to jug around the city a lil' more before this meetin'. And you know the motto."

"Slow money don't make no money," we said in unison.

Lifting three of the bags off the floor, I waited for him to grab his then we were out of the room and on our way to my truck. Keeping my guard up, I kept my eyes on my surroundings because even though a nigga was well known, that never stopped a motherfucka from trying you. You could never be too careful.

Popping the locks, I made my way to the trunk. Lifting it up, I tossed the bags inside and waited for Ace to do the same.

"Aight. I'm up," I said, dapping him up.

"Aight, mane."

"Don't be late, Ace."

"You ain't gotta say it like I'm a kid." He sucked his teeth.

"You might as well be. You heard what I said tho'. I gotta go. Eight o'clock, Ace," I reminded him.

Jumping back behind the wheel, I turned up my music and was on my way. I had a couple more stops to make and I was losing daylight hours fast.

* * * *

Checking the address again to make sure I was in the right place, I eased off my baby blue Ducati and took my helmet off. Sending Ace a text, I made sure he was in position.

Me: Ready?

Ace: I stay ready!

After getting confirmation, I made sure my pistol was safely tucked on my hip. Making my way to the front of the building, I saw the busted windows that decorated the front and that shit put me on edge. What kind of plug wanted to meet in abandoned buildings and shit?

Twisting the doorknob, I walked in the building to find it empty. Checking my watch, I saw that it was five 'til eight. I'on know what kind of shit this nigga was on, but the longer I waited, the antsier I became. Glancing down at my watch a few minutes later, I didn't even get chance to look at the time good before the clicking of heels came from somewhere in the building.

Click

Clack

Click

Clack

The closer the person got, the louder the noise became. Attempting to adjust my eyes in the darkness, I could make out someone coming my way, but I couldn't see the face.

Whipping my nine off my hip, I switched the safety off and aimed in the direction of the person.

"Yo, who dat?" I called out.

"Is that how you greet every person you want to work with?" the softest voice I had heard in a minute asked.

Stepping into the light, I tried to see the face that matched the voice, but the big ass hat and shades that she had on blocked my view.

"Work with? That ain't tellin' me who you is, mane. I'on know what kind of games you playin', shorty, but I'ma need you to gon' because I got business to handle," I told her, waving her off.

Blowing out an aggravated breath, she snatched her hat off and looked at me with annoyance before pinching the bridge of her nose.

"What makes you think that I'm not who you're meant to meet?" she asked, raising her eyebrow.

"You a lil' too pretty to be playin' drug dealer, ain't it?" I smirked, reaching out and pulling her shades off her face.

The eyes that bore back into mine had a nigga's heart thumping. I know that shit sound soft as hell, but it was the truth. Shorty was bad as hell and I couldn't think about anything else other than how her lips would form in to the perfect O shape, screaming my name.

"Don't touch me," she threatened.

"Or you'll what?" I teased.

The smirk that spread across her face caught me off guard. When she spun around and round house kicked the back of my leg, my shit buckled and I went down. Grabbing my arm and twisting it back, I dropped the gun I was holding and she had my wrist bent so far back, if I moved the wrong way my shit would snap like a twig. Pushing my body to where I was lying flat on my chest, she stuck her heel in the side of my face and applied pressure.

"Now do I have your attention?" she snarled. "You should have learned this in the streets, but I guess not, so let me re-educate you. Never underestimate your opponent. Just because I don't look like I can hurt you, I could slit your throat before you can blink an eye, or steal your lunch money without you noticing.

I am who I am for a reason. If you would have shut your pussy lickers for two seconds, I would have introduced myself and we could already have this meeting over with. You wanted my blessing to move in the streets with my product, but the answer is no.

You can continue to move how you've been doing thus far, but let me warn you, Hamin Shakespeare. I am the last enemy in the world you want because you won't see me coming," she threatened before letting my arm go and taking her foot off my head. "This meeting is over." And with that, she turned around to leave.

Pulling my body up to my knees, I rubbed my wrist to ease the soreness and brushed the dirt off my clothes. Standing to my feet, I watched in awe as she strutted out the building, her heels clicking the entire time.

Lil' mama was something else and any other person, I probably would have grabbed my gun and sent two straight through their chest, but not her. Nah, there was something about shorty that I just had to see for myself. And the crazy thing about it was, I didn't even know lil' mama's name.

CHAPTER THREE

Empriss

*E*verything about this country bumpkin rubbed me the wrong way. When I walked into the warehouse, I had every intention of giving him my blessing and when I walked in, his looks alone had my kitty thumping uncontrollably. I was ready to give him all the coke he felt that he could move, and me, for him to have his way with. Judge me all you want, but I haven't felt a man's touch in over six years, and he had me ready to take it there until he opened his mouth.

How could someone so fine open their mouth and change your whole entire mood? I know someone loved a dude that talked to them any kind of way and roughed them up because they felt like that was love, and I was all for having an alpha male, but I wasn't for the double standard shit. And I could see it in his eyes that he felt that a woman was put on this Earth to cater to men, but that wasn't me. He would just have to find someone else to supply him because I refused to do it.

My heels clicking against the pavement alerted my driver of my return. Quickly opening the back door of my Phantom, he stepped to the side and extended his hand out to help me get in. Once my feet were tucked in safely, he closed the door behind me and made his way to the driver's seat.

"Where to Ms. Reed?" he asked.

"Find me the closest bar. I need a drink bad," I instructed, taking off my hat and laying it on the seat beside me. Staring out the window as we drove, I took in the city and realized how much I missed it here. Cuba was great and all, but there was nothing like home. The thought of it gave me mixed emotions. I could only come here like a mistress in the night. Never to be seen or heard, and before the sun rose, I had to be gone again; all because I was on the run for something I didn't do.

In six years, I was still no closer to finding out who killed Jaiyce than I was the day I got arrested. It wasn't fair, but regardless of it all, this was my new reality. I was no longer the young girl that fell in love with her high school sweetheart. I was now the heartless queen pin that everyone feared but no one saw. The murderous bitch that vowed to kill every person that made me into what I am. The lost soul that vowed never to love again. And the one that would never be able to roam the streets of my city ever again carefree, because someone had stolen that from me.

Feeling the car come to a stop, I looked up to see us pulling into a parking spot in front of this hole in the wall looking spot.

"Do I need to come in with you, ma'am?" my driver questioned.

"No, Luke. I think I can handle it on my own. If I'm not out in an hour, then by all means, come inside to look for me," I said, pulling my long hair back out of my face and up in to a simple bun. I secured it the best I could, without a mirror, with two chopsticks I had in my purse.

"Yes, ma'am."

Opening my own door, I placed my feet on the ground and rose to my full height. Adjusting my blazer jacket, I made sure that I had my clutch in my hand and was ready to down some drinks. I was never allowed to just be myself while I was under Javier's watchful eye, so even if for tonight only, I was going to let my hair down. I would only be young once.

After getting searched for weapons, the bouncer let me walk in. Since it was still early, it was pretty dead in here and that was fine by me. I was just trying get a few drinks in my system and go before the Friday night crowd showed up. Easing my body onto one of the empty bar stools in the corner, I placed my clutch on the bar and checked my surroundings.

"What can I get for you, beautiful?" the bartender asked. Turning around to face her, I admitted to myself that she was a pretty girl. Maybe twenty-two at the most.

"Can I get mango Cîroc on the rocks with a splash of orange juice, and two shots of tequila silver?"

"Sure thing, I'll be right back."

Within two minutes, she was placing my two shots in front of me along with two limes and a salt shaker. Knocking back both shots, I bit into one of my limes and licked my hand before pouring salt on it and licking it off.

Handing her back the salt shaker, I pulled my drink that she set in front of me close to me and thanked her. A song I had never heard before played through the speakers. Nodding my head to the beat, I snaked my body in my seat as the alcohol started to take its course. I couldn't remember the last time I had drank for fun, if ever, and I was feeling it.

What was supposed to be a drink quickly turned into five. A little after ten, the bar came to life and was packed wall to wall with people. The music was loud and the people were hype, and I loved every minute of it.

When Drake's "Controlla" came on, something took over me and I had to get up out of my seat. Making my way in the middle of the dance floor, I moved my hips to the beat and let the music take me away. Feeling someone get behind me, I never missed a beat as I continued to slow wind my hips like I was born and raised in the islands.

I think I'd lie for you

I think I'd die for you

Jodeci "Cry for You"

Do things when you want me to

Like controlla, controlla

Yeah. Like controlla, controlla

"Ma'am. I think it's best that we go!" Luke yelled, trying to be heard over the music.

"It's okay, Luke. I'm just havin' fun."

"Ma'am, please. I don't want anything to happen to you," he insisted.

"I think you heard what she said, mane. She say she good right here where she at. Ain't that right, shorty?" the guy I was dancing with asked me smiling showing a bottom row full of gold teeth.

Immediately disgusted, I rolled my eyes and straightened myself up.

"I think he's right. I should get going," I told the stranger.

"We was just havin' fun. Fuck this nigga and dance wit' a real nigga," he said grabbing my arm preventing me from walking away.

"I think shorty said that she was good," I heard a voice say from behind me.

The look of fear that flashed through the stranger's eyes caused him to let my arm go and try to take a few steps back.

"My bad, Ha. I didn't know she was wit' you," he apologized with his hands up.

"Now you know," someone answered from behind him, reaching back and punching the guy in the face.

In a matter of seconds, the club was in a full-blown frenzy, and people were trying to move out of the way to keep from getting hit. In the midst of all the fighting, shots rang out, causing me to duck down.

Pop!

Pop!

Pop!

"Come on, shorty, we gotta go," Hamin said, grabbing me up and escorting me outside, shielding my body with his. Looking back over my shoulder, I saw Luke following close behind us and I breathed a sigh of relief because I would feel horrible if anything happened to him because of me.

Pushing his way through the club, he kept my body protected as best he could with one arm. Once we made it outside, he practically dragged me to his truck.

"You good, shorty?" he finally asked, giving me the once over.

"I'm fine," I answered, straightening myself as best I could. The liquor was still coursing through my veins, and it had me thinking irrational as hell. Staring up at him, I admired him. Hamin stood about six feet two, a solid 215 pounds with a peanut butter complexion. What made my mouth water was his head full of waves and the full beard that graced his face. He reminded me of the IG model, Rashad J, but that much sexier.

"You gon' keep undressin' me witcha eyes or you gon' say somethin'?" he asked, smiling down at me, showing off his perfect white teeth.

"Huh?" I heard myself ask, but the words weren't registering in my brain yet.

"You a sexy lil' somethin', ain't it?"

"Wait. What?" I giggled.

"I said you a sexy lil' somethin', ain't it?" he repeated.

"Ain't it? What does that even mean?"

"Shit, that you sexy," he told me, licking his full lips.

Letting my mind drift off, I imagined his tongue gliding across my body until it found my honey pot. Clearing my throat, I shook the thoughts from my head.

"Ms. Reed, we really must get goin'. You have a flight to catch,"

Luke said, bringing my attention back to the present.

"Right. I gotta go. Um… thanks," I said to Hamin.

"Call me Ha. Does this mean that you gon' reconsider my proposal?" he asked, licking his full lips and giving me a full body scan.

"No. My answer still remains the same."

"Damn. Das cold. Well, will I see you around?" he questioned.

"I doubt it," I replied, turning on my heels and walking toward the car with Luke following close beside me. Putting a little extra twist in my hips, I gave Hamin an eye full and something to remember me by, because he would never see me again. After tonight, my thoughts of missing the city would quickly go away. If I never saw Memphis again, it would be too soon.

CHAPTER FOUR

Hamin

I sat back in the corner and watched baby girl out on the dance floor for a little minute. The way she moved her body had me questioning what type of female she was under the sheets. Something about her had me wondering more and more about her, even after she flipped a nigga the way she did.

I had enough of sitting back and letting other niggas push up on her, so I started to make my way across the club to bring her back to my table when I saw some big burly looking nigga whispering in her ear. At first I thought it was her man, but once she waved him off and kept dancing, I realized that he wasn't. I didn't decide to step in until that lame ass nigga grabbed her arm, and Ace's crazy ass decided to do the rest by stomping that nigga out for disrespecting me.

He may not have disrespected me intentionally, but he touched something that I wanted, and I was a very territorial nigga. I wasn't sure who started shooting, but them niggas was gonna feel me when I finally figured out who the hell it was. Digging my phone out my pocket, I checked my phone to see I had three missed calls from Ace.

Hitting his number, I opened the door to my Rover and hopped inside while I waited for him to answer.

"Aye, mane, where you at?" he screamed in my ear.

"Pullin' up by the door. Come on. You know them boys gon' be here in a minute."

"One."

Hanging up the phone, I hit the locks as he was coming out the door. Jogging around my truck, I waited for him to get in good before hitting two wheels coming out the parking lot.

"What the fuck was that, Ace?" I asked once we were a safe distance away from the club.

"Whatcha mean?"

"You ain't have to stomp that man out like that."

"Shit, what was I 'posed to do? That mane was in violation so I handled that shit accordingly," he answered with a slight shrug.

"Whatever, fooly."

"Who was that bitch that you was cakin' wit?"

"Shit, to be real witcha, I'on even know shorty name," I admitted, shaking my head at the thought of her feisty little chocolate ass. "That's the plug."

"Her? I ain't believin' that shit. She don't look like she'd bust a grape in a fruit fight."

"Shit, that's what the fuck I thought 'til she flipped my big ass," I told him laughing at the memory. Don't ask me how she did it and I'd never admit that to no one else in my life, but shorty reminded me of

Nala when she flipped Simba's ass on *The Lion King*.

"Damn, you let shorty flip you?" He laughed uncontrollably.

"Let her ain't the right word to use, but I couldn't stop it either." I told him joining in on the laughter. "She ain't fuckin' wit' me tho'. Like on everything, mane, she straight up told a nigga that she wasn't fucking wit' me and I couldn't have her product, so I'on know what we 'bout to do," I admitted with a wave of my head.

Our old connect was under surveillance with the feds, and I couldn't fuck with him no more. That's why I worked so hard to get in touch with some people I knew that copped from Javier. Only thing was, Javier was supposed to be retired and he told me he would put me on his protégé. I guess that's where lil' mama came in to play.

As if a lightbulb went off in my head, I knew exactly how to get what I wanted. If lil' mama refused to work with me, I would go back to the nigga that put her in my presence the first time: Javier. I ain't have shit to lose at this point.

"You know we can't keep fuckin' wit' Raul. That shit like sendin' the feds right to our door steps wit' a target on our backs, mane," Ace stressed.

"We got about thirty-five keys left to play wit'. We can extend them out for about another two weeks or so, but that's still gon' be cuttin' it close. I got a plan tho," I told him.

"And what's that?"

"If shorty don't want to fuck wit' us, I'll go to the one person I know she'll listen to... Javier."

29

"You think it's gon' work?" he asked, lighting his blunt and taking a pull from it.

"To be honest with you, my nigga, it has to; 'cause if it don't, we fucked."

I wasn't thinking about the possibility of my plan not working. Shit, failure wasn't an option. Shorty already told me no when I asked, so if he turned me down too, a nigga was fucked. And I mean with no Vaseline. Turning up my radio, I listened to the words as I went over my plan in my head again. Shit had to pan out; if it didn't, I wasn't sure what my next move would be. I had to make this move my best move; wasn't no plan C.

* * * *

Getting up bright and early the next morning, I said a quick prayer to Allah and prayed that everything went in my favor today. Heading into the bathroom, I washed my face and brushed my teeth, and took a leak before going back into my room to grab my phone from my charger.

Taking a deep breath, I dialed the number I had written down on the piece of paper and waited for the call to connect. The phone rang repeatedly before it suddenly stopped.

"Do you know what time it is?" the thick Cuban voice asked.

"Javier, I know it's early. I'm sorry, but I needed to speak with you," I explained.

"You seemed to have pissed my daughter-in-law off pretty good. Why should I listen to anything you have to say?"

"I know I did, and again, I'm sorry. It wasn't my intent. But wit' all due respect, you know just as well as I do that goin' into business wit' me is good for both of us. I'm a natural born hustler, and I get my money by any means," I boasted. All my diplomatic talk flying out the window.

"That's one of the things I admire out about you, Hamin. You don't take no for an answer. It makes you both admirable… and stupid. But you are correct, though; you would be a good asset to the team. However, I'm not the one you need to convince," he reminded me.

"Is there any way that you can set up another meeting?"

"In Memphis? No. there's no way that Empriss will step foot back in to the States so soon. If you want to see her, you will have to fly to Havana."

"Cuba? You want me to fly to Cuba?"

"Yes. Cuba. Is that a problem?" he questioned, and I could hear the skepticism in his voice.

"Nah," I answered.

"Good. You have until the end of the week to plan your trip. I plan to see you at my villa by dinnertime on Saturday evening. And, Hamin?"

"What's up?"

"If you blow it a second time, you won't be leaving Havana alive," he warned before hanging up the phone in my ear.

Jumping up to my feet, I wasn't worried about his threat. A nigga was just happy that he agreed to set up another meeting with shorty and in the process, I learned her name.

Empriss, huh? I thought.

Well, little did Ms. Empriss know, she gon' love a nigga by the end of my three-day visit to Havana. Now, all I needed to figure out was how the hell I was gon' be ready to leave for Havana in a week; but come hell or ice water, I had to make up for the first meeting. I was ready to get to this money, and she was my key to doing so.

CHAPTER FIVE

Empriss

The flight back to Havana was long as ever and I couldn't wait to make it home to my prince. Even though I was only gone for a night, it felt like ten. Since I didn't travel often, it was hard to be away from my baby for more than a few hours, because the fear of getting locked up and never seeing him again always played repeatedly in my head.

It was a little after five in the morning when my plane landed, and I was ready to get in my bed. But I knew that I wouldn't be getting sleep any time soon because JJ would be up and ready for breakfast within the next hour or so.

The ride from the air strip to my villa was a short one. Maybe ten minutes at the most, and unlike how you heard most queen pins lived, I tried to live as normal as possible. I didn't want an extravagant house that had more rooms than I could count. We didn't live ridiculously flashy, but we lived extremely comfortable.

The house had six bedrooms, three and a half bathrooms, and I had an in-law suite attached. There was a living room, a sitting room, and JJ had a game room out of this world, but what I loved about the house most was my kitchen. I had a five-star kitchen with all stainless-steel appliances. Before my arrest, I was going to culinary school. It had always been my dream to be a chef. I was born to cook.

On the outside, the backyard was huge. Javier had taken it upon himself to get the backyard turned in to a soccer field when JJ turned three, and my baby had been playing ever since.

Using my key to unlock the door, I tried to be as quiet as possible without waking anyone, but that was short lived when Lady and Rocky came rushing around the corner before knocking me to the ground.

"Okay. Okay. I missed you guys too." I laughed.

My blue noses were my babies and I treated them like they were.

"I'm sorry, ma'am. By the time I tried to catch them, it was too late," my bodyguard, Esteban, apologized.

"It's okay; they just missed their mama, that's all." I smiled. "Luke is outside, you can go out with him now."

"Yes, ma'am."

Esteban and Luke were the only two bodyguards that I felt I needed. Luke went with me when I traveled out of the state, and Esteban stayed to protect JJ and Mrs. Lucinda when I wasn't around.

"Come on. Let's go see what good we have in here to eat," I told the dog, making my way in to the foyer.

"MAMA!" I heard JJ yell from the top of the stairs, causing the biggest smile to spread across my face.

"Mijo. I've missed you so much," I said, giving him a kiss on the top of the head while he wrapped his arms around my legs.

"I missed you too. Guess what Papa told me while you were away."

"And what was that?" I asked absentmindedly while I grabbed two steaks out the fridge for Lady and Rocky.

"He said that if I was lucky, that you'd marry and have me a little brother or sister soon." He bounced in his chair excitedly.

"Did he now?"

Javier had been trying to convince me for years that I needed to date and have more kids, but my excuse was always the same. I couldn't move on with my life if Jaiyce's killer roamed free, walking the Earth. I just wouldn't feel right. I would never be able to have real happiness knowing I failed him.

"Yes. So, is it true? Am I going to have a little brother or sister soon? Having a dad would be nice too."

"Jaiyce. We talked about this," I started, and the once happy expression he wore on his face was soon replaced with a sad one.

"I know, Mama. You loved my dad, and you can never love anyone the same," he told me.

"That's where you're wrong. I loved you a million times more than I could have ever loved him, but right now isn't the right time," I explained.

"I know, Mama." He sulked, jumping off the barstool.

"Wait, where are you going? I'm making your favorite. Chocolate chip pancakes."

"No, thanks. I'm not hungry. I'm going back to bed," he mumbled, dragging on his way back up the stairs.

Watching him until he disappeared, my heart grew heavier. I knew JJ wanted us to be a complete family, but I didn't see that in the cards for us. I didn't lie to him when I told him that I could never love another man the way I loved his dad. I knew he didn't understand right now, but when he grew older and fell in love, he would. A husband and a baby wasn't in the cards for a woman like me. JJ was all I had and I was okay with that.

* * * *

The next few days went by so fast that most days I didn't know if I was coming or going. Today was just like any other Saturday; JJ had his soccer games, or futbol, as they called it here, and we had dinner with Papa. All day he had been calling to make sure that I was coming over to eat, and it was starting to get weird.

Papa never bothered me about Saturday dinners, but today he insisted that I leave JJ with Lucinda because we had business to discuss, which wasn't something we normally did. We handled business religiously Monday through Friday, but Saturday was reserved for family dinner and games, and Sundays were church and one-on-one time with my prince. So for him to be throwing off the normal rotation of things was kind of rubbing me the wrong way.

Instead of letting it throw me off my square, I did as he said. I dressed down in a cute black bodycon sundress and a cute jean shirt to throw over it. My hair was pulled back into a tight bun with my silver chopsticks safely tucked in place in the center of it. Deciding on a pair of some knee-high gladiator sandals, I slid my feet in them and was ready to go.

Hearing a slight knock on my bedroom door, I gave myself another once over in the mirror and I was satisfied with my outfit. I was comfortable and I was still cute/casual at the same time, so it worked.

"Come in," I called out, applying a thin coat of lip gloss to my lips.

"The car is waiting out front for you, ma'am," Esteban told me.

"Okay, here I come," I told him, grabbing my black Marc Jacobs clutch and heading out of the room and down the stairs to the car. When we pulled up to Papa's, there was a red Cadillac in his driveway that I hadn't seen before.

Dismissing it, I figured the car had something to do with the business that we were supposed to be discussing tonight over dinner. I wasn't sure who exactly it was, but I wasn't really dressed to meet new people. However, this was how I dressed every Saturday, so this would just have to do.

Being escorted to the door by Luke, I thanked him and made my way inside once we made it to the door. I could hear voices coming from the dining room area, but instead of heading there first, I made a pit stop in the bathroom to wash my hands and check my makeup. First impressions were everything to me, so I needed to make sure that I looked as presentable as possible since I wasn't in my normal business attire.

Leaving out of the bathroom, I stood in the hallway listening to Papa laugh and joke with this mysterious person. There were only a handful of times in my life that I could remember Papa laughing, and each of them had something to do with JJ in some shape, form, or fashion, so to hear him laughing with a stranger piqued my interest.

Curiosity getting the best of me, I walked towards the dining room with my head held high as if I owned the place.

"Sorry I'm late, Papa. If I had known we were having company, I would have dressed in something more appropriate," I spoke, making my presence known. Walking into the room, I saw Papa standing over on the far side of the dining room, closer to the sitting room next to the bookshelf where he kept his baseball card collection. The stranger had his back toward me, but I could feel his aura all the way from where he stood. It screamed "respect me."

"It's okay, mija. I'm sure our guest doesn't mind. Do you?" Papa asked, touching the gentlemen on the shoulder.

"Not at all. Nice to see you again, Empriss," he spoke, turning around a flashing me his Colgate white smile. The look of confusion must have shown through on my face because he winked at me.

"Hamin?"

"The one and the only," he stated with a smirk.

This shit could not be life, I thought, swallowing my spit.

CHAPTER SIX

Hamin

The look of shock and confusion on Empriss' face had me wishing that I had a camera. Her face was priceless.

"What are you doing here?" she asked frozen.

"I was invited," I replied.

"Yes. I invited Hamin to come visit us since you were so eager to shoot down his proposal, I was interested in hearing what he had to say," Javier told her.

"Well, I'm sorry you wasted your time coming here, but like I told you at the bar, my answer is still no," she sassed.

"What bar?" Javier questioned, losing all hint of laughter in his voice. Instead, it was replaced with a stern icy voice that could chill bones.

"Papa... I... I mean," she stuttered. When Javier started making his way from where I stood around the table, the fear in her eyes grew and she started taking small steps back towards the door.

"Did you go to a bar while you were in the States?" he questioned, grabbing ahold to her arm and applying pressure.

"Yes, sir," she answered meekly.

Everything unfolded so fast I barely had time to blink. Reaching his hand back, he used all his might to slap her, sending her flying to the floor.

Slap!

"Do you understand how stupid that was! You not only put yourself in danger, but me as well. Do you forget who we are? Do you forget that we are fugitives of the US? If you go down, you don't go alone. You're dragging me along with you, and I will not be a prisoner in some American jail cell. Do you understand me?" he shouted, his Cuban accent coming through stronger with each word he spoke.

"Yes, Papa," she answered, her voice trembling while she gripped the side of her face.

"Get out of my face and go clean yourself up," he commanded with a wave of his hand.

"Yes, Papa," she whimpered. Pulling herself off the ground, I watched as she kept her face down and made quick steps out of the dining room headed to do as she was told.

This wasn't the same girl that I met back in Memphis. The confidence she once possessed was gone and she turned in to a shell of herself in Javier's presence. I wanted to speak on him putting his hands on her but I had to remind myself that I was a guest in his house and this was his country. I wouldn't make it out this room alive if I opened my mouth.

"Where's your bathroom?" I asked, setting my glass of cognac I was nursing, down on the table.

"Down the hall and three doors to your left, and make sure you wash up good. Dinner will be on the table when you return," he said smiling at me, turning back into the person he was right before the incident unfolded.

"Sure thing."

Swaggering out of the room, I put a little pep in my step. I followed his directions and made my way down the hallway but not in search of a bathroom. Careful not to make too much noise, I listened until I heard soft crying coming from behind one of the doors.

"Open up, shorty," I said, knocking lightly on the door.

"Go away."

"Come on, mane. I know you ain't 'bout to make a nigga beg. It's either you open the door or I'ma kick this bitch in. You got three seconds to decide. One. Two. Thr—" before I could get the word fully out my mouth, I heard the locks clicking.

Easing the door open far enough to slide my body inside, I closed the door behind me and locked it. Turning to give her my full attention, a nigga's heart broke watching the tears stream down her face as she tried to gently dab the blood off her swollen lip.

"Sit down, shorty. Let me," I told her, setting her down on the toilet.

Uncuffing my sleeves, I pulled them back as best I could, careful not to get my suit jacket dirty. Grabbing one of the rags from out the closet, I put it under the warm water. Turning back around to face her, I kneeled in front of her and took her chin in my hand and pressed the warm rag to her lip.

"Owwww. That stings," she hissed, snatching her head away.

"It's gon' to. Either you take the little bit of pain now or you gon' feel it tomorrow when it really swells up. Now hold still," I said, looking her in the eyes.

When I put the rag back to her lip, she winced a little underneath my touch, but she took the pain. Never taking my eyes off her, when she finally let her eyes meet mine, I didn't blink. I silently challenged her with my eyes to look away.

Reaching my free hand up, I used it to wipe the tears off her cheeks and out of the corners of her eyes. I wasn't sure what it was, but a part of me was ready to take her with me, guns blazing. I wanted to protect her.

"What did he mean when he said y'all were fugitives of the state, shorty?" I asked, keeping my eyes trained on her.

"We can never go back to the US. Not freely anyway," she admitted, casting her eyes to the floor.

"Stop doin' that."

"Doin' what?"

"Lookin' away like you ashamed. I've only been around you three times and I've never see a chick more sure of herself. Yo' ass was even confident as hell when you was drunk as fuck dry humpin' the hell out of a stranger." I laughed.

"We were not. We were dancing."

"You call it dancing. I call it fuckin' witcha clothes on. That's not my point tho'. What I'm sayin' is, you walk around like you the shit because you is. You should never let a man put his hands on you. Pops or not," I educated her.

"He's not my father," she admitted.

"I know that already. That's what makes it ten times worse. Like you told me, you are who you are for a reason, right?"

"You act as if I own the world or something," she said, locking her eyes back on mine.

"You do. It's ya world, ma, I'm just tryna live in it," I told her honestly.

The silence that filled the bathroom created this tension between us, but it wasn't awkward. Shorty had me ready to bend her over this toilet and fuck my way into her inner circle. I had every intention on trying to finesse her out that pussy so that she would be begging me to move her dope, but at this moment, that shit didn't even matter.

I was trying to fuck her to replace her pain with pleasure. Her tears into moans. I meant what I said, it was her world. I just wanted to be a part of it.

"We should really get back out there before he comes lookin' for us." She cleared her throat, standing to her feet putting me eye level with her kitty.

Standing to my feet, I allowed my body to purposely brush against hers. My dick was harder than a diamond and it was pressing against her stomach.

"Um. Could you back up so that I can move?"

"I'on bite, ma. I may nibble a lil' bit, but not enough to hurt," I teased, backing on up a little.

The lust in her eyes mirrored mine, and if she kept looking at me the way she was, I was about to give her exactly what the fuck she was looking for. Eight inches of it.

Instead of replying to my slick remark, she tried to suppress her smile and started towards the bathroom door.

"Hamin?" she called with her back still facing me and her hand on the knob.

"What's up shorty?"

"Thank you."

She didn't give me time to respond because she strutted out of the bathroom and just like that, she was the woman I met again. You would never know that she had just got slapped down ten minutes before now.

Shaking my head, I laughed lightly to myself, fixing my suit jacket back to the way it originally was. This was gon' be one interesting ass cat and mouse game, and even if I wanted Empriss bouncing up and down on top of me, I still had business to handle. I needed to move her product, and no matter what it took to make that happen, I was willing to make that sacrifice.

* * * *

The dinner went off without a hitch when we walked back into the room, and my plan to win Javier over was working out in my favor. And even though Empriss showed interest behind closed doors, she was back to being stubborn right afterwards. This shit was going to be harder than I thought.

"Thank you again for having me, Javier. We gotta do this again soon," I told him, shaking his hand.

"We'll have plenty of time over the next few weeks that you're here. You'll be staying with Empriss."

"WHAT!" Empriss yelled.

"My guest is your guest so you will treat him as such."

"Look, a nigga ain't tryna impose or no shit like that," I told them, the hood coming out of me in a matter of seconds.

"You're not. Is he, mija?" Javier asked, giving Empriss this look.

"No, Papa. Come on, you can follow my car to the house," she instructed, walking away.

"We'll meet up again later this week. You have your work cut out for you." He laughed.

"Yeah, I know." I shook my head and made my way to my rental.

I don't know who told this nigga I was staying for two weeks. I thought I was going to be down her for a few days, seal this deal, and be on the first thing smoking back to Memphis with more kilos of coke than I knew what to do with. All this other shit was not in the plan, but I guess I had to do what I had to do.

The ride back to her crib was short and when we pulled up, I had to admit it wasn't what I expected, but it was beautiful. Parking my car in the circle driveway, I grabbed my duffle off the passenger seat and met her in front of the door.

A gun cocking close to my head caused me to freeze in my tracks.

"It's okay, Esteban. He's with me," Empriss told him.

"Yes, ma'am," he answered in a thick Cuban accent, disappearing again. Turning around, I didn't see where the fuck that nigga went. A nigga could fuck around and get caught slipping out this bitch.

"Mane, you got niggas waitin' in the bushes and shit, shorty?"

"Only when they need to be." She shrugged, opening the door.

Bark!

Bark!

Bark!

"Detener!" Empriss yelled just as two big ass blue nose pits came rushing around the corner.

I don't know what she said to them, but they stopped immediately but didn't stop looking at a nigga like I was a prime steak and they hadn't eaten in months.

"Rocky. Lady. Bed," she commanded.

"They don't know you and if you leave my eyesight for too long, they will try to rip your throat out. So don't get any ideas," she warned.

"I'on know what type of niggas you used to dealin' wit, ma, but I'on take pussy. That shit come a dime a dozen for a nigga like me."

"What are you trying to say?"

"Exactly what I said. Yo' pussy ain't that special for me to want to take it; so don't trip, ya safe wit' me," I told her truthfully.

I wasn't that type of nigga. If I had to take the pussy, then that meant that it wasn't meant for me.

"I hear you," she sassed with an eyeroll.

She could get an attitude all she wanted, but I wasn't that pressed for her or her pussy. Yeah, I wanted it, but I wanted her dope more, so I was thinking with my big head, not my little one.

"JJ!" she called up the stairs.

Within a minute, a little boy came running down the stairs. He was a handsome lil' nigga. He had a head full of curly hair and a smile that could light up the whole room.

"Mama!" he smiled, running up to her until he noticed me standing behind her, and the smile instantly fell from his face. "Mama, who is that?"

"JJ, this is Hamin. He's goin' to be staying here for a couple of weeks," she explained.

"What's up, lil' man?" I greeted sticking my hand out to give him dap.

"What's up?" he mimicked, trying to put a little bass in his voice. "How come you gon' be stayin' wit' us for a while?"

"Jaiyce. It's not how come. It's why," Empriss corrected him.

"Okay. Why are you goin' to be staying wit' us for a while?"

"I just got some business I have to handle witcha moms, that's all," I answered.

"What kind of business?"

"Jaiyce!"

"He aight. Leave the lil' nigga alone." I told her before turning back to him. "I just got grown up business to handle. What about you? You play sports or anything?"

"I play futbol."

"Oh, that's what's up! I was the star QB on my college team," I bragged.

"QB? What's that?" he asked, jumping up on the barstool.

"You must not be any good if you gotta ask me what it's called," I joked, taking the seat beside him. "Maybe tomorrow we can go outside and toss the ball around and you can show me whatcha got."

"No, silly. We play futbol wit' our feet." He giggled.

"Ohhhh. You mean soccer. Nah, a nigga ain't no good wit' his feet."

Feeling eyes on me, I looked up to see Empriss shooting daggers in our direction. Not paying her no mind, I winked at her and finished my conversation with lil' man.

"How old you is, lil' nigga?"

"I'm five." He smiled, showing off his pearly whites.

"Jaiyce. It's time for bed," Empriss told him, interrupting.

"But Mama, it's the weekend," he groaned.

"And I said, it's time for bed. Go, JJ. Now!"

"Yes, ma'am. Goodnight, Mama. Goodnight, Hamin," he told us, jumping down with a sad expression on his face.

"Call me Ha," I told him with a wink.

"Okay. Goodnight, Ha," he said, his smile coming back in full effect.

Watching him bolt up the stairs, it made me think about when I had a lil' one. I wasn't getting no younger, but the streets was nowhere to raise a child, and I couldn't risk something happening to my seed because of some shit I did. I'd never be able to live with myself.

Feeling her eyes still on me, I turned around to see her with that same stuck up ass expression on her face like she smelled something.

"Why you got that fucked up ass look on yo' face like yo' ass been suckin' on lemons and shit?" I asked' giving her my undivided attention.

"Don't come in here and talk to him like you know my son. You will stay the fuck away from him," she seethed.

Confused, I could tell she was serious, but I didn't see nothing wrong with me having a conversation with the young nigga. It was just that a conversation.

"Shit, you act like I was tryin' to sell the young nigga crack or somethin'. It was an innocent conversation. You trippin.'"

"Stay away from my son, Hamin. He doesn't have a father and I don't need you tryin' to play one to him. We're fine just the way we are."

"Whoa nah. Nobody said anything about tryin' to be his dad. I'on even know the lil' one like that, so how could I want to be his people?

You lookin' too much into shit, and for you to have to convince me that y'all good without a man in y'all life only proves that you not.

I'on know what type of shit that you and yo' baby daddy got goin' on, but that ain't got nothin' to do wit' me. Hell, wit the way you be actin', I wouldn't want to be round ya ass either. I'm convinced that ya ass either bipolar or crazy as fuck."

"Fuck you!"

"Oh, I'd love to. Maybe that'll calm down some of that bitchy attitude thing you got goin' on." I laughed. "But on the real, fuckin' you is bad for business. You too hot and cold for me. Just point me in the direction of the room I will be stayin' in and I'll stay outcha way for the next few weeks," I told her, grabbing the duffle bag and standing to my feet.

I wanted Empriss, yes, but not enough to deal with her bullshit. What I felt was purely animalistic, but I needed to stay in her good graces for the next few weeks so I could get this product. I could tell now this shit was gon' be a lot harder than I thought, and I prayed that I made it back to Memphis in one piece.

CHAPTER SEVEN

Empriss

Flopping across my bed, I kicked off my shoes and stared at the wall in silence. For all the years that I had known Javier, he had never put his hands on me. Not once. To have him hit me in front of Hamin made it that much worse. Letting my mind drift off to Hamin, I allowed myself to smile the way I've wanted to all night.

Something about that man was both intriguing and annoying all at the same time. One minute I was thinking about kissing his soft lips, and the next, I wanted to slap the smug smirk that he seemed to always wear off his face.

The fact that he would be in my house for the next couple of weeks put me on edge. I could keep up the façade as best I could, but I knew with time, he would break down my defenses and I didn't need the distractions. Pushing Hamin to the side in my mind, I thought about JJ and how his face lit up while he talked about sports. I could tell that he enjoyed having a man around the house, but this wasn't a man that he needed to attach himself to.

Prying myself from the bed, I made my way out of my room and down the hall to JJ's room to apologize. He may have felt that I was being harsh, but I was just trying to protect him. Stopping short just before his door, it was cracked and I could hear voices coming from inside.

"I'm sorry about my mom. She doesn't mean to be so mean," I heard JJ say.

"Yo' mama a grown woman. You ain't gotta apologize for her. You may call her mean but she not. She just tryin' to protect you," Hamin answered.

"Protect me from what?"

"The world. She protectin' you the best way she knows how, and that's by keepin' you from getting' too close to strangers. Especially strange men like me."

"But I don't think you're strange," JJ admitted.

"I may not be strange to you, but you still don't know me. I may not have intentions on hurtin' you, but there may be people out there that would hurt you to get to her. It's not meant for me to explain to you, and one day maybe ya moms or ya dad will explain to you what I mean."

"I don't have a dad," JJ told him in a soft sad voice. "My mama said he died before I was born."

"Damn. I mean, dang. I'm sorry to hear that. I wouldn't know what to do without mine. He showed me so much. He made me in to the man I am today."

"Well I won't have anyone to show me how to be a man."

In that moment, my heart sunk. JJ may have only been five, but he was smart. Like my grandma used to say, he acts like he's been here before. I was about to burst in the room and wrap him in my arms and never let go, but when Hamin started to talk again, I decided against it because I was curious what he could possibly say to him.

"Listen to me, you don't need anyone to show you how to be a man. Being a man is something that comes from within you. Don't get me wrong, my dad showed me how to be a man through example, but it was up to me to apply what he showed me and create my own lane.

You know what type of man that you want to be already. You just gotta stay on the right track and it will happen. You gon' do alright, lil' nigga. Now get some sleep before yo' mama hear us and come kick both our asses." Hamin laughed.

"Okay. Good night, Ha," JJ told him.

Ducking quickly into the guest bedroom, I leaned against the wall until I didn't hear his footsteps anymore. Once the coast was clear, I turned back around and headed back to my room. What Hamin told JJ replayed in my head over and over.

You don't need anyone to show you how to be a man. Being a man is something that comes from within you.

Being a man was something that I couldn't teach him and as hard as it was to admit, he needed a male figure in his life that was a positive influence on him. I could teach him how to treat a woman and have respect, but the sad reality is, a woman couldn't teach a little boy to be a man.

* * * *

Waking up early the next morning, I handled my morning routine as normal. After I washed my face and brushed my teeth, I slid my silk red robe over my body and headed downstairs to the kitchen. I could hear light humming and I already knew it was Mrs. Lucinda.

"Good morning, Lulu," I greeted, kissing her on the cheek.

"Good morning, mija. You're up early. It wouldn't have anything to do with that fine man that came parading down here, would it?" she asked, giving me the side eye.

"I have no idea what you're talking about," I told her, clearing my throat.

"Sure you don't." She laughed and continued to mix the batter she had in the bowl. "What's bothering you?"

"Who says something's bothering me?" I asked, sitting down at the chair close to the island.

"The look on your face says it all. Now spill it."

Taking a deep breath, I tried to gather my thoughts as best I could to put them in to words.

"I overheard Hamin telling JJ that he didn't need anyone to teach him how to be a man. I want to be mad because he didn't have any business being in JJ's room, but I can't be," I admitted.

What Hamin told him bothered me, but he told him something I would never be able to explain to him; and I didn't know which part bothered me more— The fact that I couldn't or that Hamin did.

"You don't want to hear it, but I will tell you like I have been since

Jaiyce was a baby. He needs a father."

"His father is dead."

"What does that supposed to mean?" she asked, setting the bowl on the counter and staring at me.

"It means that he doesn't have a father and he never will," I replied with a shrug of my shoulders.

"Why deprive Jaiyce of having a father all because his isn't in the picture? So you will both be lonely and miserable for the rest of your lives because his father died?"

"We're not lonely or miserable."

"A blind person can see it. Don't let your fear keep you from exploring something wonderful. Just because you don't agree with his lifestyle, Hamin being around may actually be good for him. It's not like what the two of you do is that different," she pointed out.

"But—" I opened my mouth to answer but Hamin stepping in to the room stopped me. I watched as he lifted his shirt to wipe the sweat that was leaking down his face exposing his abs.

I must have been staring again because Lulu's snickering snapped me out of my trance.

"Good morning again, Mrs. Lucinda. Empriss," he greeted, giving me a wink.

"Good morning," I said, keeping it short.

"I will go upstairs and wake JJ," Lulu said, dismissing herself from the room and leaving us alone.

The tension between us was thick, but I wouldn't necessarily say that it was uncomfortable. There seemed to be hostility pouring out of me, but calmness coming from him. It was unnerving.

"Why you always lookin' like that?" he questioned, leaning against the wall.

"Looking like what?" I sassed.

"Like that," he pointed. "Yo' face always curled up like you smell somethin' sour or some shit."

"Maybe I do."

"You too pretty for all that shit to be honest, but if you wanna walk around lookin' sixty at thirty, be my guest," he said, pushing himself off the wall and walking around the island headed toward the staircase.

Stopping behind my chair, his cologne caught in my throat and my breath became ragged. I could feel him bend forward and his beard tickled my neck as his lips came close to my ear.

"I think you just need some dick in yo' life. Maybe if you wasn't so damn mean to me, I would bless you, but I'on think you ready for all that," he whispered in my ear before laughing and walking out the room.

Temporarily closing my eyes, I tried to ignore the familiar thumping between my legs before quickly regaining my composure.

"Be ready in thirty or you're getting left!" I shouted up the stairs behind him.

"Yes, ma'am." He chuckled before I heard a door open and close.

The sooner he went back to Memphis, the better. I wasn't sure how much more of this little game I could play, and the bad part about it was he hadn't even been here a full day. Letting my head fall back, I took a deep breath and stared at the kitchen ceiling. This would be a very long two weeks.

CHAPTER EIGHT

Hamin

Completely ignoring Empriss, I walked into the guest bedroom without a care in the world. Stripping down out of my sweaty clothes, I made my way to the adjoining bathroom and turned on the shower. Working out in the morning always helped me keep a clear mind, and I wasn't going to let anyone throw me off my square, not even baby girl.

Stepping in, I let the hot water cascade down my head and back. Saying the Al-Fatiha, I continued to say it until I felt myself at peace. After my third time reciting it, I lathered my body up with soap before rinsing off and getting out. Bypassing the towel that was on the counter, I let the air hit my body as I went to find my clothes for the day.

The weather in Havana was nice as hell, and if I was here for pleasure instead of business, I knew I would be walking around like any other tourist that came to visit. Deciding on a pair of light denim jeans, I paired it with a black collared Polo and my low Polo loafers. Grabbing a pair of briefs out of my duffle, I bent down to put them on when a gust of wind hit my body, causing my dick to go stiff.

"Hamin! I told you to be ready in…" Her words were cut off when

I stood to my full height.

Her eyes grew the size of saucers as she took in my body. I knew I wasn't an ugly nigga by a long shot, and the way she was staring at my dick let me know that she appreciated more what I had to offer.

"You need somethin'?" I asked to fuck with her.

"Ummm… Yes. I told you to be ready in thirty minutes and you still haven't made it downstairs," she said clearing her throat.

"It's just a dick, shorty. You can look at it." I laughed.

"Just put some clothes on and meet me downstairs," she sassed, turning on her heels to walk back out of the room.

In two long strides, I was behind her, blocking her between me and the closed door. Placing one hand on the door to keep it closed, I wrapped the other hand around the front of her body and placed it on her stomach.

"What are you doing?" she asked, her voice trembling.

"Shhhhh," I replied, turning her around and picking her up pressing her body against the door.

Wrapping her legs around my waist, I could feel the heat radiating from between her legs.

"Hold on to me," I demanded in a low voice before I let my hands fall from underneath her. Using my now free hands, I pulled up the sides of the sundress she had on.

"What are you doing?" she asked again but never took her hands from around my neck, nor attempted to stop me.

Reaching the thin fabric she called panties, in one quick flex of my fingers, I ripped it and exposed her bare kitty. Walking her over to the bed, I laid her body down and hovered over her, careful not to place my weight on her tiny frame.

Rubbing my fingers up and down her folds, I smirked to myself, feeling her juices, and I hadn't even done anything yet. I already knew that Empriss was feeling the kid, no matter how hard she tried to fight it, but the way she was leaking only confirmed what I already knew.

"Damn, ma. I ain't even fucked you yet."

Putting the head of my dick at her opening, I held on to it while I teased her clit with the head. I watched the hunger on her face as she began to rotate her hips. Applying a little pressure, I allowed the head to slip in a little but prevented the rest from going in. Keeping the tip in, I made circular motions against her clit until the look on her face scrunched up, telling me she was about to explode.

Without warning, I stopped and stood to my feet before walking back in the bathroom to get my rag that I left draped on the edge of the tub.

"What the fuck, Hamin!" Empriss snapped, walking into the bathroom looking like an enraged bull.

"What?" I said, acting confused.

"What the fuck was that? Why do all of that if you had no intentions on taking it there with me?"

"You not ready for that, ma. You like me right now, but you'll hate me again later. This was just my way of proving that you want me more than you let on. Trust me, when the time is right, I'll give you exactly what you lookin' for. You will beg me to put all this dick in your life," I told her, winking.

"Fuck you, Hamin!"

"Oh, I plan to."

"Ughh!" She huffed, storming out the bathroom and out the room, slamming the door behind her.

Laughing to myself, I shook my head before heading back in the room to finish getting dressed. I had every intention on fucking Empriss into oblivion, but first thing first, I needed her to agree to supply me and then I'd give lil' mama all the dick she wanted. No questions asked.

After I was dressed, I headed back towards the kitchen where I heard all the noise coming from. Stepping into the room, the first thing I saw were those big ass dogs staring at me like I was a slab of meat and they couldn't wait to stick their teeth in me.

"Hamin!" JJ yelled, excited, running towards me.

"What's up lil' man?" I smiled giving him dap.

"Lulu cooked breakfast. Come eat with me," he said, tugging my hand to pull me toward him.

"What we eating?"

"Pork sausage. Turkey bacon. Cheese grits and blueberry muffins," Lulu said setting a plate in front of me.

"I don't eat pork. I'll take a piece of turkey bacon and a muffin though. Oh, and a glass of orange juice if you don't mind." Feeling eyes on me, I turned around to meet Empriss's angry stare.

"What's wrong wit' you?"

Rolling her eyes at me, I suppressed my laugh because I knew what the hell was wrong with her, and her spoiled ass wasn't hurting me with her little fucked up attitude. She'd be alright.

"Here you go, Hamin."

"Call me Ha. Thank you. I gotta go handle some stuff witcha moms but later, you gon' show me what you got in soccer?" I asked, turning toward JJ.

"Futbol," he corrected.

"Okay, well futbol then."

"Sure." He nodded with a mouth full of food.

"Cool. I'll see you later. See you later, Lulu," I told her, standing up to down my glass of orange juice, then grabbing my muffin and taking a bite of my bacon. "Come on, grouchy," I told Empriss, swaggering off. I was ready to get the day started. Before it was all said and done, I would be the distributor in Memphis. You could bet your bottom dollar on that.

* * * *

"How many keys can you move a month?" Empriss asked, pulling into the gate of a compound.

"A hundred. Maybe more. Depends on the grade of the coke." I shrugged. I could sell water to a goldfish if given the task. That's what being a hustler meant. It was all about the gift of gab.

"You will move a minimum of 120. If you prove yourself worthy and don't fuck up, you will get more coke and more grounds to move it on," she said, stepping out of the car and strutting towards a storage unit.

Keying in a code and placing her thumb on a scanner, the locks clicked and she bent down to lift the door. Pushing the door up, she walked in and the lights automatically popped on. There had to be at least fifty crates in the room. Walking over to one of them, she slid the top off and I came face to face with the whitest coke I had seen in my lifetime.

"Get one out," she commanded.

Doing as I was told, I picked up the brick and looked at the dove that was stamped on the wrapper. Pulling out my pocket knife, I set the brick back down before looking up at Empriss.

"May I?"

Simply nodding her head, she watched my every move as I made a slit in the side of the brick and scooped a little out with the knife. Rubbing the residue across my gums, they went numb instantly and a smile spread across my face so wide that I knew I looked like that Cheshire cat off Alice in Wonderland.

"How much?"

"A hundred and twenty keys at seventeen-five a piece. Your first set will run you 2.1. You can sell these easily at twenty-five a piece or set deals for the ones that buy more. The choice is completely up to you. As long as I get my cut when it's time to re-up, that's all I care about. Do we have a deal?" she asked, turning into the boss bitch I met that day in the warehouse.

"Mane, you damn right we got a deal," I told her, extending my hand out to shake hers.

"Good, and another thing. I only deal with you. You are the only one that sees me. You are the only one that knows my name. To the rest of your crew, to the rest of the world, Empriss doesn't exist. You pay for them. You move them. I expect you in Havana every month on the fifth for your package. The first time you're late or you don't show up, I will mail your nuts to your mother until I get my money. I didn't make it to the top because of my looks. You underestimated me once. Don't make the mistake and do it again," she said, leaving out of the storage unit, leaving me alone with my new best friends.

Eyeing the crate full of keys, I couldn't do shit but thank Allah for blessing a nigga. I had the buyers and now I had the coke. I was about to have the whole Memphis on smash, and it was only right that I had Ace right there along with me. Empriss didn't know it yet, but I was about to be the best distributor that she had ever seen.

I was ready to move more coke than a little bit, and as my nigga Lucci said, I got the keys to the streets and the city. Might as well call me the mayor.

CHAPTER NINE

Khalid

I had been calling this nigga Hamin for the past few days only to get my calls ignored like I was some kind of bust down. I don't know what type of shit this nigga was on, but he was starting to piss me off. Hitting the number on my phone, I paced the floor waiting for my call to get answered.

"Hello."

"Ace. Where the fuck is Ha at? He ignoring my calls like I'm some kind of hoe he fuckin' or somethin'," I snarled.

I wasn't pressed for this shit with Hamin. I wasn't scared of him or this looney tunes ass nigga Ace, but if he knew like I knew, he needed to get back at me with a quickness.

"If the nigga treatin' you like you a hoe then you probably is," he answered.

"Yo, who the fuck you talkin' to my nigga?" I asked, looking at my phone.

"Obviously, the nigga on the other end of my phone. Shit, I ain't keepin' that nigga in my back pocket, so you gon' have to wait for that nigga to hit you back or keep blowin' his phone up, but callin' me wasn't the best option."

"You got some steel nuts, you know that shit?"

"Never get it twisted. I'on work for you, my nigga, and you ain't shit but another body to add to my list. Ha ain't in my back pocket, and even tho' I know where he at, it ain't my business to tell. So, I'on know what to tell you, mane," he said.

"I ain't even 'bout to take it there witcha. If you talk to that nigga, tell him I'm lookin' for him," I said.

"I won't," he replied before hanging up the phone in my ear.

Rude ass motherfucka.

Something was off about that nigga. He looked like the type that tortured kittens as a kid or some shit. Weird ass nigga.

Dialing his number again, I really felt like a hoe that was trying to get in touch wit' her cheating boyfriend, but this shit was beyond my pride. Hamin had the reputation to know everything about everybody, and he always knew his enemy, and I needed him to help me find mine.

I had sent one of my workers Jeffrey after this Cuban cartel princess by the name of Rebekah. I had been searching high and low for her. I didn't handle competition well and this bitch was bad for business. From what I heard, she had some of the purest cocaine this side of the south had seen, which meant her pockets were getting fatter and mine were getting slimmer.

I had just gotten word that he was able to get close to her a few weeks back before I lost communication with him. A couple days later, his body was delivered to his doorstep with a note attached to him that read:

"Seek and you shall find."

"Yo," the voice answered on the other end of the phone.

"Nigga, where you been?" I snapped.

"I must have lost the memo, are we fuckin'?"

Clenching my jaws together, I tried to keep my temper at bay because these niggas were really trying me today.

"Between you and ya punk ass homeboy, y'all testin' me in the worst way. I must got 'try me' stamped on my fuckin' forehead or somethin' cause both y'all niggas on it today," I said sucking my teeth.

"Mane, move around wit' all that rah rah shit. You called my line for somethin' and I know it ain't coke, so what's up?" he asked.

"I need you to find someone for me."

"How much?"

"If you find her, I'll give you fifty g's. If you can point me in the right direction, twenty-five."

"Wooh. I'm not in town right now and I won't be back for a minute. It'll have to wait until I make it back and handle my business."

"How long is a minute? I ain't got time to be waitin' around for you to move. I need this shit done ASAP," I told him.

"I wasn't askin' ya permission," was what I heard before the phone let me know he'd hung up.

"Man, fuck!" I yelled in frustration, throwing my phone against the wall.

Falling back into my desk chair, I thought of all the different ways that I wanted to kill both of these niggas, but whether I wanted to admit it or not, I needed their services so they would breathe another day. But before it was all said and done, I planned to put two through both them niggas' domes if it was the last thing I did.

CHAPTER TEN

Empriss

The decision to supply Hamin came completely out of left field for me. I wasn't sure if I agreed because I knew he was a beast in the streets, or if it was the fact that my body reacted to him in ways that I haven't felt in a long time. I hadn't been with a man since Jaiyce died six years ago. I may have let someone lick it once or twice, but that's as far as it went.

Hamin had me hot and bothered in more ways than one, and the longer he stayed in my presence, the more I found myself longing for him. I wanted to hate him because of his disrespectful ass mouth, then in the next breath, I wanted him to kiss me with the same lips he popped that fly shit from. The shit was confusing and I just needed him back in Memphis and far away from me.

Like now, I was tossing and turning in my bed trying to ignore the urge to sneak in his room and let him fuck me senseless. Getting frustrated, I threw my head back and decided to head to the kitchen to grab something to drink to cool my hot-in-the-ass self down some.

Hearing a noise in the hallway, I grabbed my baby .22 from my

71

nightstand table and flung the door open, ready to shoot.

"Whoa, man," Hamin said, throwing his hands up and dropping the bowl of ice cream he had on the floor.

"Dammit, Hamin. You're cleaning that shit up too," I sassed, stepping over it and proceeding downstairs.

"You ain't tryin' to help me? You the one made me drop the shit in the first place," he answered, his voice right behind me as I made it down the stairs.

"I'll give you the stuff to clean it with, but I'm not getting on that floor to clean it."

"Yeah, I would hate for your ass to poke out any further in them lil' ass shorts you got on," he commented, rubbing his hand up the back of my thigh.

Sending a chill down my spine, I practically jumped out of my skin but tried to keep my composure as best I could.

"Ain't no one around but us. You ain't gotta act like you hate me. I won't tell anybody you feelin' ya boy," he teased pulling on my shorts.

"Stop it, Hamin," I whined.

"Or what?"

Spinning around on my heels, I gave him a slight smirk before taking off running towards the kitchen. Within two long strides, I was in his arms and he had me penned against the wall looking down at me.

Even if I wanted to deny it, I couldn't. Hamin Shakespeare was one fine specimen of a man. His beard did something to me, and the way he licked his full lips when he looked at me had me wondering what they felt like.

"Fix us another bowl of ice cream and I'll be back once I clean this mess up," he breathed out.

Nodding my head up and down, I waited for him to move so that I could do as I was told. Winking his eye at me, he leaned up a little to let me past and smacked me on the butt to give a little encouragement.

Grabbing two spoons out the kitchen drawer, I placed them on the counter before grabbing the Homemade Vanilla Bluebell ice cream container out the freezer. Standing in front of the counter, I opened the tub and used one of the spoons to scoop some in my mouth. I don't care what anyone said, Bluebell had the best ice cream, hands down. I was so consumed in my thoughts that I didn't hear Hamin come back in to the room until he lifted me up and placed me on the counter.

Pulling the barstool over, he sat between my open legs and opened his mouth for me to give him some.

"Un-uh. I am not ya mama," I told him, waving my head, eating another spoonful.

"That's cold. Gimme," he said reaching out for mine.

"Nope," I said, popping my lips.

"Gimme." He stood to his feet.

Shaking my head from side to side, I went to get another spoon when he snatched it out my hand.

"Why you gotta be so difficult all the time?" he asked.

"I'm not difficult."

"Nah, you right. You just a bitch," he stated matter-of-factly.

Before he was able to get the spoon up to his mouth good, I slapped the shit out of him.

"Who you callin' a bitch?"

"Did you just slap me, shorty?" he questioned rubbing his jaw.

"Did you call me a bitch?" I countered.

Staring daggers at me, my heart started to beat out of my chest and his stare made me want to back down, but I would never give his ass the satisfaction. How dare he call me out my name and then stand here like everything was supposed to go back to normal.

"Move," I snapped, pushing him out of my way and jumping off the counter.

I didn't have to deal with this bullshit, and especially not in my own house. Who the fuck did Hamin think he was? This reminded me why I couldn't stand his black ass in the first place. His mouth got the best of him and he didn't think about what he said before he spoke. The shit was both a turn off and turn on.

"Where you think you goin', Empriss?" he asked, gripping my wrist.

"Let me go, Hamin!" I yelled, snatching my wrist away and looking dead at him.

"When was the last time you had some dick?" he asked, catching me off guard.

"What?"

"For real, shorty. You act like you ain't had none in a minute or something. What, ya lil' boyfriend ain't fuckin' you right?" he joked, but I didn't find that shit funny at all.

"Who is and who ain't fuckin' me right isn't any of your damn business."

"Oh, that means that nigga ain't on his job. Let daddy show you how it's done." He smiled, pulling my body towards his. "Tell me you don't want me and I'll leave you alone. You can act like you don't want a nigga all day long but..." He paused, reaching out to rub two of his fingers against my kitty through my shorts. "...I bet she soaks for a nigga every time I come around," he finished.

"You'll never know," I sneered.

"Oh, I won't?" he asked, picking me up and carrying me into my living room and setting me down on the couch.

"Stop it. You're just going to tease me again," I told him, trying to push him off me.

"Tell me you want me and I'll give it to you," he replied, kissing down the side of my neck.

His lips were as soft as I imagined they would be. The feel of his lips on my skin and his massive hands roaming my body, I was slowly melting in his grasp.

"Tell me," he insisted, letting his hand roam up my thigh until he reached the waistband of my shorts.

Tugging on them, I lifted my hips slightly to let him pull them off, but kept my eyes closed because I didn't want to see his face when he discovered that I wasn't wearing any panties.

"Sssssss," I heard him hiss. "Tell me I can have it. I told you I didn't want it unless you begged me to take it there wit' you and I meant that," he told me before pulling away to stand up again.

"Wait, don't. I want it," I whispered, opening my eyes.

"I'on understand whisperin'. You gotta tell daddy what you want."

"I want you," I admitted.

"Nah, I ain't convinced. What you want?" he challenged, standing to his feet, pulling his shirt over his head.

"You."

All pride aside, I wanted Hamin, and even if it was for one night only, I wanted him to be mine. Better yet, I needed him to be, and I was about to show him just how much. Sitting up, I pulled him closer to me, tugging on the drawstring of his grey sweats.

"You sure that's what you want, ma?" he asked, looking down at me.

Waving my head up and down, I kept tugging until the knot was gone. Taking a deep breath, I eased them off and came face to face with one of the biggest dick imprints I had seen in a minute.

Six years is a long time to remember the stroke game of your ex, but from what I could remember, Hamin was longer and thicker, and that shit caught me off guard.

"You scared yet?" he smirked.

"No. I meant what I said, I want you," I told him again.

"Be careful what you wish for, shorty."

Rising to my feet, I kept my eyes trained on him as I pulled my shirt over my head, freeing my c-cups. His eyes traveled my body lustfully. Taking a step closer, I stood on my tiptoes and pressed my lips against his.

Gripping my hips, he crushed his lips into mine and deepened the kiss. The way his tongue moved inside my mouth pushed me over the edge and I lost the little bit of composure that I had.

"You know once we take it there, you mine, right?" he huffed.

I wasn't paying attention to anything that was coming out of his lips. The only thing I wanted to hear was the sound that my noni would make as he stroked me.

"Just shut up and fuck me." I demanded. And he did just that.

For close to an hour, Hamin did things to my body that I never experienced and took me to places that I had never been. I had so many orgasms that each time I climaxed, I felt I couldn't go anymore until he took me over the edge again.

My eyes were so heavy, the whole time he carried me up the stairs, I felt like I was floating on clouds. Feeling my body being laid across my bed, I rolled over in the fetal position ready to let sleep consume me.

"Un-uh. I ain't done wit' you yet, shorty," Hamin told me just before he took my body on another journey. Looks like I wasn't going to sleep any time soon, and I welcomed it.

CHAPTER ELEVEN

Hamin

I was back in Memphis one happy man. Not only had I secured the deal being Empriss's new distributor, but baby girl was finally warming up to me. It didn't matter how hard she acted in front of Javier and during the day, she was my little freak at night. I was cool letting her be the queen in the streets but when it came to us, there could only be one king to the castle and that was me.

Parking my car in front of Ace's apartment building, I hopped out and hit my locks before heading inside. I never understood why Ace still chose to live in the hood after everything we had accomplished. We came a long way from the young niggas on the block slanging rocks.

Knocking on the door, I bounced my leg waiting for him to open the door. When he didn't come to the door or call out within the first thirty seconds, I brought my fist down on the door and knocked on that bitch like I was the police. Call a nigga impatient because that's exactly what it was.

"Who the fuck is it!" he yelled from the other side.

"Open the door and find out, my nigga," I retorted.

Swinging the door open, this nigga looked pissed off but I ain't give a fuck. Should've opened the door faster.

"Hamin, make me kick yo' ass. Knockin' on my fuckin' door like you done lost yo' mind and shit."

"Kill the noise, my nigga. Did you get up wit' Khalid?" I asked, taking a seat on his living room couch.

"I ain't talked to that bitch since he called my phone last week lookin' for you. I'on even know why you keep that nigga around. Something ain't right wit' that nigga," he said, stroking his beard.

"Look who's talkin'," I replied, raising my eyebrow.

Ace didn't have no room to be saying that someone else wasn't right. This nigga is the only person I knew that would shoot a nigga for stepping on his shoes. The nigga was two shades from being a fucking psychopath, and a wild cannon all the way around, but he was my nigga so I kept his crazy ass around.

"What? I know I ain't right in the head. Hell, I welcome that shit. The hoes ain't complainin'," he told me, sticking his tongue out.

Shaking my head, all I could do was laugh because the nigga was telling the truth. Hoes loved that nigga's dirty drawers. Crazy and all.

"Enough about that nigga tho'. What happened wit' that chocolate broad?" he asked, leaning forward.

"Shit, we in that thang. We gotta move more weight than what we used to, but ain't no doubt in my mind that we gon' get this shit off. You ready for this takeover, my nigga?"

"Is a pig pussy pork?"

"These niggas ain't gon' know what hit them. They think our name ringin' bells now. Just wait. Nigga, I'm tryna make they ass sick." I said laughing.

My hustle wasn't something that could be duplicated very easily, and now that Empriss had basically handed me the keys to the streets, literally, that I needed to take over, I was one step closer to stacking my chips and getting out the game for good.

"Let me go holla at this nigga, Khalid, tho' before he have a bitch fit. I'm up," I told Ace, standing to my feet.

"Aight."

"And another thing, Ace… we 'bout to be on and shit gon' get more hectic by the day. We moving more weight and gon' be seein' way more dough. Livin' in the heart of the hood might not be the best look," I pointed out.

"Look, I'm my own man. I live and breathe this hood shit. If a nigga gon' come for what's mine, he gon' have to come to my neck of the woods. That suburb shit ain't me. I'on wanna walk out my door and see old bitches walkin' down the street gettin' in them miles, or Tom's ass mowing his grass.

Put me in the gutta where you see bums on every corner, hoochies walkin' around showin' off that pussy print, and hear gunshots in the mornin'. Broken glasses and fiends. That shit soothes a nigga like me. My ass would fuck around and cause a massacre if I left the hood. This shit just who I am," he said with a straight face.

"I feel you on that. All I'm sayin' is, if they come for you, they

81

come for me. You can't be a boss nigga with a million-dollar work ethic and a dollar bill state of mind."

"I got that red dot waitin'. I got me. You just handle you."

"Aight," I told him, leaving the conversation there.

If Ace was more comfortable in the hood, then that was on him. I would never forget what we grew up in, but at one point, a nigga had to want better; however, Ace would have to want it on his own. I couldn't do the shit for both of us.

* * * *

The ride to Khalid's put me way out of my way home, but apparently, this nigga was gon' keep blowing up my phone until I came by to see him. Sitting in his living room, I looked around at the pictures on the wall and they reminded me of that nigga Tommy's house off *Belly.*

"It took you long enough to get back at me," Khalid said, stepping in to the room.

"I was busy. What's up? You said you got a job for me," I told him, getting straight to the point.

There was something about Khalid that rubbed me the wrong way. The only reason I dealt with him was off the strength that his money was always good. We were in the same line of business and he copped his keys from me, and from time to time, he paid me for information. Most niggas didn't know it, but I was a jack of all trades when it came to this hood shit. If it needed to be done, I could always find a way to make it happen. If it was dope, I could move it. If it was a person, I could find them. If it was a hit, I could make 'em disappear.

That was one of the reasons that I knew Javier wasn't about to let me slip through his fingers. I was too valuable to a nigga like him.

"Yeah. My uncle put me on to this chick that is a threat to our family and our empire. Her name is Rebekah and shorty seems like a ghost. Every time someone from our end gets close to her, they end up disappearing without a trace. Last we heard, she was somewhere out of the country, but I don't know exactly where," he said, causing me to look at him like he had three heads.

"Okay, so let me get this right. You want me to find a chick that you don't know where she is? Do you at least know what she looks like?"

"That's the thing. The picture I have of her is over eight years old and its gritty. Like I said, lil' mama a ghost and she has been for a long time," he told me, handing me a tattered picture.

Inspecting the picture, I could make out a gritty face, but it wasn't enough for me to go on. This shit was like the blind trying to lead the damn blind. How he want me to find someone and he couldn't even show me what the bitch looked like.

"You killin' me, mane. For all this, the price just went up. If by some miracle I find this broad, you payin' me extra to bring her to you. That shit is just a finder's fee," I told him.

"That's bullshit, Ha. You tryin' to rob a nigga."

"Fair exchange ain't robbery. Either you want this shit done or you don't. The shit don't matter to me."

"We'll talk 'bout it once you find her," he said.

"Oh, that's funny. This shit wasn't up for debate. Take it or leave it. Either you want her found or you don't. Hurry up and make your decision because I got shit to do," I said, ready to make my exit.

"Aight. Find her."

"I thought that's what you'd choose. I'll call you when I got somethin'. That's exactly what that means, my nigga. Don't be blowin' up my shit. When I find somethin', you'll know," I told him before walking out the door and out the house.

Finding this Rebekah chick was gon' be a lot harder than I expected it to be but there hasn't been a person walking this Earth that me or anyone I was affiliated with couldn't find. If she was out there, trust me, I'd find her. She could run, but she couldn't hide.

CHAPTER TWELVE

Ace

$\mathcal{W}$hen Hamin called me telling me what Khalid wanted, something about the whole situation made my stomach hurt. I didn't give a fuck what anyone said, Khalid was a snake. They could call me crazy and demented all they want because I would shoot a nigga in broad daylight and torture someone in front of they moms, but at least I knew what type of nigga I was.

Niggas like Khalid were the ones you had to watch out for at all times. He appeared to be your closest friend, and he would be plotting your downfall the whole time.

My phone dinging let me know that I had a text. Grabbing it off the arm of the couch, I looked at it before a smile spread across my face.

Ha: *Get them bags ready. We leave in the mornin'."*

I'on know how Hamin pulled it off, but he got lil' mama to work with us and I was more than ready to make them birds fly. I thought the shit was too good to be true until he let me test the coke we were

85

about to be selling, and I swear I died and went to heaven.

I could spot pure coke from a mile away, and that shit was on point. Sending out a text to my second in command, I let him know that I would come around to make drops to all the spots later on today to last them until we got back with more. A nigga had never been outside of the States, so I was more than ready to see what them Cuban bitches had to offer. I was trying to put some of this country dick in they life, ya feel me?

* * * *

"I told you, I only deal with you Hamin. Who the fuck is this?" the brown-skinned chick from the club yelled pointing her finger in my direction.

"This is Ace. He wit' me," Hamin told her.

"He gotta go. Thank your friend because he just cost you your life," she told me before I heard the cocking of pistols and these big burly ass bodyguards she had surrounding her pulled out on me.

"Unless you want one of these niggas to lose an eye, you might want to tell them to lower they shit," I told her, never moving a finger to go towards my gun. I just kept my hands folded in front of me close to my belt buckle.

"You sure about that? There are four of them and one of you," she said, cocking her head to the side with a slight smile dancing on her lips.

"I bet I drop two of these niggas before one can let off a shot," I told her. "And then after I fuck up all these niggas, maybe I can give you somethin' to tame that fucked up little attitude you got." I blew a kiss at her.

"Watch it, my nigga," Hamin said, giving me a dirty look.

"Okay, I guess no dick for you then. Too bad, you don't know what you missin', shorty. Now back to what we was talkin' about. You want to be responsible for these two lovely gentlemen losin' an eye all because you on that fuck shit. I ain't ya enemy, ma, and I promise you don't want me as one," I told her, staring at her. I may have chuckled but wasn't shit funny.

When she didn't tell them to lower their guns, I took that as the hint that lil' mama was trying to call my bluff, so I gave her exactly what the fuck she wanted. Letting my hands go to either side of my belt, I snapped my wrists out and sent two knives flying on either side of her, catching the two niggas close to her in their right eye. Spinning around, I pulled my gun off my waist and put it to the head of the nigga behind me while the other one put his gun to my head, causing Hamin to pull out his.

"Arghhhhh," I heard the two niggas on the floor scream out.

"Say the word, ma'am, and I'll drop him now," one of them said to her.

"Wrong. Pull that trigga and I'll know every thought you've ever had. I'on mind brain splatter," Hamin threatened through gritted teeth. "Empriss, tell this nigga to drop his gun or I'ma drop him and I put that shit on my unborn kids."

"Let's see if you can pull your trigga before I shoot your homeboy," I said, taunting the one I had at gun point.

"Shut the fuck up, Ace!" Hamin yelled.

"Empriss, is it?" I asked, turning my head in her direction. "I'ma be honest wit' you, ma. I'll leave ol' boy stankin' right here and let Ha blow ya other boy brain's out and we'll leave this bitch like nothin' happened because let's be real, ma, you ain't gon' kill him. You might shoot me, but you need Hamin. So this shit can work one of two ways. You can test my gangsta or you can tell these niggas to put they shit away. Everybody gotta die one day and if today is my day, then so be it," I explained.

Amusement flashed through her eyes before she waved her hand and signaled for the other two to drop their guns.

"Luke. Esteban. Take Carlos and Juan to get their eyes checked out," she instructed, never taking her eyes off of me.

"But, ma'am," one of the started to say.

"It's not up for discussion, Luke. Now!" she yelled, staring at him, daring him to say something else.

"Yes, ma'am."

Tucking my gun back in my waistband, I watched Luke and Esteban help them off the floor.

"Oh yeah, and I'ma need them back once they take 'em out," I said. "Now that that's out the way and you see that I ain't no hoe, what you got to eat, a nigga hungry?"

I could see Hamin throw his hands up out the corner of my eye, but I was still looking at Empriss as she broke out in to a full-blown smile. I watched the way she looked at Hamin before turning on her heels and strutting out of the warehouse. I couldn't wait to eat this nigga alive. There was something going on between him and Empriss, and I'm pretty sure that whatever it was had his dick involved. Ain't that about a bitch.

CHAPTER THIRTEEN

Empriss

"*I* told you not to bring anyone with you," I said to Hamin later on that night as we lay in my bed.

"Ace just ain't anybody tho'. Everything I do, Ace is right there wit' me to have my back in case some shit pop off. To be real witcha, he the only nigga I trust outside of myself," he told me, running his fingers through my hair.

"Seriously? He acts crazy as hell."

"Shorty, you not the first and you damn sure won't be the last to call that man crazy. That's what makes him Ace," he told me, laughing, but I didn't find it funny.

Two of my workers were blind in one eye because he wanted to play target practice with them. I couldn't lie though; I was in awe of Ace. Not only was he a soldier that knew his way around weapons, but he was a man of his word. He didn't make empty threats. I was partially to blame because I tried to pull his hoe card, only to find out he didn't have one.

"Well, now that you got him to help you, when should I be expecting you back in my territory?" I asked, rolling over on top of him to look in to his eyes.

"I'll be back next month. Maybe before. Why, you gon' miss daddy?" he teased, grabbing around the back of my neck and inching me towards his staff.

"Maybe," I told him, giving him a slight smirk.

"Maybe, huh? Well let me make sure I give you something to miss," he replied, guiding his dick into my opening.

Moving my hips slightly, I inhaled deeply as I tried to adjust to his size. Picking up his pace, he rocked in a circular motion, making sure that I felt every inch that he had to offer.

"Ssssss. Dammit, Haminnnn," I moaned out, throwing my head back.

"Fuckkk," he groaned, matching my movements with his hand on my hips.

He started to pick up his pace and with each thrust, he hit my spot repeatedly, driving me crazy. Raising my hips, I tried to relieve the pressure he was applying, but the more I tried to run, the deeper he dug.

"Un-uh. Take that dick," he demanded, stroking me in a way that was firm and gentle all at once.

Closing my eyes shut tight, I held on while he continued to hit my spot until I felt my body ready to fly over the edge. Spinning me around in the reverse cowgirl, he leaned up and pulled my body to his chest, continuing to apply pressure to my neck.

"Hammmmiiinnnnnn," I cried out, clenching my walls as his teeth dug into my shoulder blade.

Pushing my body forward, he forced me to lay flat on the bed before laying down on top of me, sliding back into me. I didn't know what he was doing to my body, but I never wanted him to stop.

Giving me deep, long strokes, I bit into the covers as my eyes rolled to the back of my head.

"You gorgeous. You know that?" he asked, digging deeper. "This shit dangerous. Fuck, Empriss, I'm about to nut." He groaned, lifting my leg up in an angle and picking up his pace.

The feel of him throbbing inside of me as he exploded was enough to make me explode.

"I'm cumminnnnn," I cried out.

The only sound that could be heard in the darkness was heavy breathing as we both tried to catch our breath. Feeling him roll off of me, I leaned up on my forearms and stared at his silhouette.

"Is it worth it?" I asked brushing my hair out of my face.

"Is what worth it, gorgeous?"

"This. Us. You said it's dangerous. Is it worth the danger?"

"On God it is. You worth all the risk, ma. Believe that," he said, causing me to blush.

"Okay," was all I could say as I wrapped up in his arms and sleep take over my body.

* * * *

Knock. Knock. Knock.

"Ms. Reed?"

The knocking on my bedroom door caused me to stir out of my sleep. Opening my eyes, I realized that Hamin was no longer in the bed to the left of me. Glancing over at the alarm clock, it showed that it was a little after seven in the morning.

"Ms. Reed?" Luke called out again.

"Yes?"

"Um. Something came for you."

"I'll get it in a minute," I told him, easing out of bed and grabbing my robe that was draped across the ottoman beside my bed.

"I think you want to see this," he insisted, pissing me off.

Tightening my robe in front of me, I stormed towards the door and snatched it open with fire in my eyes. I was already feeling some type of way about Hamin leaving my bed in the middle of the night like I was some late-night creep, and now Luke's persistence.

"What could possibly be so important that it couldn't wait until I came to see what it is?" I questioned, not bothering to hide the annoyance in my voice.

"It's about Jaiyce, ma'am. We got another lead. I know you said don't bother you about him unless it was important, but I believe that this is," he answered, trying to keep his eyes away from my body.

"Jaiyce?" I mumbled. "Are you sure?"

"Yes, ma'am."

"I'll be out in a minute. Tell the guys they better beat me outside. We're goin' for a ride," I threw over my shoulder, as I went back into my room to hop in the shower and get dressed.

Placing my hair in a messy bun on top of my head, I adjusted my water in the bathtub. Dropping my robe, I glanced at my body in the mirror before doing a double take to stare. Hickies littered my body from the nape of my neck to my inner thighs.

I felt Hamin nibbling on me but I didn't think it was hard enough to leave marks. Turning my back towards the mirror, I looked over my shoulder to see just as many marks on my back and shoulder blades. Turning back around, I traced my fingers over the ones that graced my breast.

A small smile spread across my face as I started to have flashbacks over the way he caressed my body. Closing my eyes, I felt every curve, every stroke, every kiss and every bite. I could picture the look in his eyes when he kissed me and sucked on my bottom lip. What we had going on was truly dangerous but I couldn't deny it.

The feeling of bliss I was feeling was soon replaced with anger when I thought about how he snuck out my bed. Pushing all the thoughts to the back of my head, I focused on getting my shower out of the way so that I could handle what needed my attention: Jaiyce and his killers.

Whatever beef I had going on with Hamin would have to wait. I couldn't focus on being Empriss the lover. The switch had turned on and I was now Empriss the ruthless queen pin. Time to handle business.

CHAPTER FOURTEEN

Hamin

Stopping my stopwatch, I checked down to see my time for my mile run.

Three minutes, forty-six seconds.

Damn I was slipping. My mind was so wrapped up in getting back to Empriss that I wasn't even paying attention to my workout. Jogging the little distance to her house, I checked my watch and saw that it was almost eight. I had been out the house for a little over an hour and half and I was trying to get back to her before she woke up and realized I was gone.

Taking the front steps, I reached out to open the door but before I could put my hand on the knob, it twisted and the door opened. Coming face to face with Empriss, we locked eyes and a nigga heart started thumping.

"Where you headed to?" I asked, smiling down at her.

Reaching out to pull her towards me, she stepped back and swatted my hand, catching me off guard.

"Out. I got stuff to handle," she replied in a flat tone.

Checking out her outfit, baby girl had on an all-black pantsuit that hugged her body like a second skin, with the open suit jacket that showed off her black bra.

"Out? Not witcha bra all out you ain't."

"It's a bralette," she corrected.

"I'on give a fuck what it's called, but the point is, you not wearin' it out."

"Last time I checked, you were not my man nor were you my daddy. So, like I said, I'm goin' out. I'll be back later so we can make sure the shipment is ready," she snapped, trying to walk around me.

"Shorty, I'on know what the fuck done got in to you, but I guarantee you don't wanna go there wit' me. Either you go change ya damn shirt or I'm comin' wit' you," I told her, reaching my arm out to block her path.

"I'm not changing, Hamin," she challenged.

"Well go sit ya mean ass in the car. I'll be ready to go in a minute," I told her, letting my arm fall to my side.

"Excuse me? I didn't say you could come with me."

"I'm grown, shorty. I go wherever the fuck I wanna go. Now go sit yo' mean ass in the car like I said. I'll be out in a minute."

I didn't even stick around to see the hateful glare she was giving me. I'm not sure what the hell Javier was letting her do before I came around, but she had the right nigga. She was right, I wasn't her man or her daddy, but I was zaddy, and I didn't play that shit. My dick was entering her pussy meaning she was mine and she would respect me. End of discussion.

I said it once before and I will say it again, Empriss could be the queen in the streets all day long, and I would let shorty rock out with that, but when it came to inside the castle, she was still a queen but I was the king. I wasn't some little ass boy that she used to her convenience and told me what she was and wasn't gon' do. Shorty may not have known any better right now, but before it was all said and done, she would learn.

"Ayo, Ace!" I yelled up the steps on my way to the guest bedroom.

"What's up?" he asked, stepping out the room with his pistol in his hand ready to go. That's what I loved about him; he was trained to go, always.

"Get dressed. We about to follow Empriss hot in the ass self somewhere." I told him stepping in to the room.

"Aight." I heard him call out behind me.

It took me twenty minutes tops to wash my nuts and get dressed and I was out the door with Ace walking right beside me. Since Empriss said she had business to handle, I decided to dress in black too. Ace must have sensed some shit about to pop off because his outfit mimicked mine. Black beater. Army fatigues and black Forces. This was some shit that I could throw away easily.

Catching Empriss staring at me through the cracked window, I winked at her and blew her a kiss. Rolling her eyes up in her head, all I could do was laugh as I hopped in the passenger seat of the rental. We followed behind the town car for a good thirty minutes before we took a left and started riding through the slums.

This was the part of Cuba that they always showed on the TV, the ones where the little kids looked like they hadn't eaten in months. Or they were running down the streets barefoot, down the block, chasing the rich people's cars, looking for a handout.

Coming to a stop in front of a hut, I hopped out before Ace could turn the engine off once I saw Empriss step out the back seat. Checking the safety on my gun, I made sure that it was off before tucking it back in my lower back and stepping up. Her bodyguards positioned themselves so that they protected her on all sides, as she stepped through the sheet that acted as a door and stepped in the house.

"I'm looking for Jose," she announced in a calm flat tone.

"Jose isn't here," a lady answered with trembling hands.

"Is that right?" she asked, pushing her Chanel frames on top of her head. "My problem with that is, I got information from someone that I trust that he is associated with one that I'm trying to get to. Either you can tell me where he is or I will tear this place down brick by brick until he appears."

The venom that dripped in her tone caught me by surprise. Studying her face, there was something harsh about it. Something I hadn't seen before, and I wasn't sure if I should be impressed or a little worried.

"Please. I said Jose isn't here," the lady said.

"Fine. Tear it apart," she ordered over her shoulder, turning around getting ready to walk out the door.

"Wait. Wait. Here I am!" a man who I assumed must have been this Jose cat, yelled out, coming in to the room with his hands up.

"Jose. Please!" his moms cried out with tears staining her face.

"It's okay, Mama. I'll go with you, just please leave her alone," he pleaded in a heavy accent.

"Of course," Empriss said, smirking. Snapping her finger, Luke and Esteban snatched Jose up and put a burlap sack over his head.

Sliding her shades back over her eyes, she turned around and strutted out the room and back to the car like she hadn't just snatched somebody in broad daylight.

"Mane, that broad crazy," Ace said, taking the thought right out of my head. "You better watch out for her ass before she chop yo' dick off in yo' sleep and feed it to you for breakfast." He laughed, following them outside.

Waving my head side to side, I gave Jose's mama one last look before reaching in my pocket and handing her the knot I had on me. Flinching away from me, she started to speak in Spanish and from the tone of her voice, I could tell she was cursing me out.

"I'm not tryin' to hurt you. Take the money. It's fine, I promise," I told her, taking a step closer with my hand still extended out towards her.

Hesitantly taking the money out my hand, she stared at it in shock before breaking down in tears.

"Thank you," she told me, smiling.

Tipping my head toward her, I left without another word. That shit may have seemed strange for me to give her money after Empriss snatched her son. It wasn't like I was giving it to her as payment or as an apology, but because she needed it. I couldn't dare think of my mama staying in a place like this. Shit, whether my pops was taking care of her or not. And if Jose couldn't afford to help his moms out for whatever reason, I would, so I did. Simple as that.

"What took you so long?" Ace asked, bringing the car to life when I eased into the passenger seat.

"I had to handle somethin'. Just follow shorty so that we can get outta here," I told him, looking out the window.

A feeling I couldn't explain came over me and I wasn't sure what it was, but I could tell that whatever Empriss wanted with this Jose cat was gon' rub me the wrong way.

* * * *

"What do you know about the murder of Jaiyce Ortis?" Empriss asked, sweat dripping down her forehead.

"I told you already. I don't know a Jaiyce," Jose stuttered through busted lips.

"Wrong answer."

Gripping the brass knuckles on her fingers, I watched Empriss cock her arm back and put all her strength in the blow that she delivered to the side of Jose's head. She had been beating him for the past twenty minutes and his answer hadn't changed one bit.

"WHAT DO YOU KNOW ABOUT THE MURDER OF JAIYCE ORTIS?" she screamed.

The look in her eyes was almost demonic and shorty looked straight up possessed. Jose's sobs filled the room and for once in my life, I felt sorry for a grown ass man pleading for his life. If I felt he was guilty, then I wouldn't have had a problem with her beating his ass to a pulp, but even a blind person could see that this nigga didn't know what the hell she was talking about. Everyone but her.

Taking the gun off my hip, I walked over to where they stood. Empriss was so caught up in screaming at him that she didn't see me until it was too late.

Pffff! Pffff! Pffff!

Emptying my clip, the silencer I had on kept the gun sounds off, but watching the bullets rip through his chest was enough to make me turn my head.

"What the fuck was that! I wasn't done talkin' to him!" Empriss barked, turning her anger towards me.

"You call that shit talkin', shorty? You asked that man the same fuckin' question over a hundred times, and he gave you the same answer a hundred times! The man didn't know shit! Wasn't no point in watchin' that man suffer when you was just gon' kill him anyway, so I put that nigga out of his misery," I snapped.

"That wasn't for you to decide! He was my only lead, and now you took that shit away from me."

"HE DIDN'T KNOW ANYTHING, EMPRISS! Everyone could see that shit but you. What? You ain't notice how uncomfortable everyone was lookin' in this bitch? I'on know what the fuck it's gon' take you to come to grips wit' it, shorty, but let me spell this shit out for you. Jaiyce is dead and that nigga ain't never comin' back."

Fire stung the side of my face and before I could stop myself, my reflexes kicked in and I caused her the same pain that she caused me.

Smack!

Guns cocking filled the air and I didn't even give a fuck; if these motherfuckas was gon' shoot me then they would have to shoot me in my back because I was out this bitch.

"Come on, Ace," I said, swaggering out of the warehouse and towards the car.

I wasn't pressed for this shit. If she wanted to spend her life trying to avenge a nigga that had been dead for over six years, then by all means she could do that shit because it was her prerogative. But I wasn't about to stick around and watch her cuckoo ass beat innocent people in the process.

I would continue to move her coke faithfully every month, but wasn't no need in me pursuing anything else with her. I would never have her heart. Another man already laid claim to that, and wasn't no way in hell I was competing with a ghost.

CHAPTER FIFTEEN

Ace

*P*eeling my banana, I sat back and watched Hamin storm around the room like a raging bull. This nigga was throwing shit, mumbling to himself, and cussing as if the shit was going out of style.

"But why you so mad tho'?" I finally asked.

"What you mean?" he asked, stopping in his tracks.

"Exactly what I said. Why you mad that she huntin' down the motherfuckas that killed ha nigga? I bet money that if someone killed the bitch that you was in love wit' that you'd be goin' to the ends of the Earth to find they ass, so why is it so bad that she doin' it?"

"That's not the point. She beatin' innocent people, and for what? Huh?"

"In her eyes, the nigga wasn't innocent, and like I said, if the roles was reversed, you wouldn't give a fuck if you had to snatch a nigga grandma, and you know that shit is punishable by death off top; you'd do it. It's more to it than that and you know it. It's because you fuckin' her, ain't it?" I asked, taking another bite of my banana.

"What?"

"What, you thought a nigga ain't notice? The pope could stand in front of y'all and tell y'all fuckin'. Hell, if you wasn't fuckin' her, I would've damn sure tried my luck wit' her stuck up ass."

"Watch it."

"Nigga, I ain't about to watch shit. This my mouth and I say what the fuck I wanna say. And like I said, I would've tried to fuck her mean ass if you already wasn't but since you are, that mean she's off limit... but that shit is neither here nor there. What I'm sayin' is, you can't get mad at lil' mama for doin' somethin' you know damn well you would do too.

If she want to kill everybody between here and San Jose lookin' for the people that killed that nigga, then that's on her. You ain't got no right to tell her who she can and can't kill. That's not for me or you to judge. Again, why are you mad?" I asked, looking at him.

"She's a female, Ace! It's different for me, you right. I could go out and run the streets and paint the city red because I'm a man. That's what men do. It's my place to rule wit' an iron fist. It's okay for me to rip through motherfuckas like they deer meat. BECAUSE THAT'S WHAT NIGGAS DO!" he yelled, spit flying with his every word.

"Shorty puttin' her life on the line and for what? For a nigga that's been in the dirt for six years? What's gon' happen when she snatch the wrong nigga and they kill her ass? Who gon' be the one to carry on for her? Who, JJ? A five-year-old little boy that ain't never had a father. I'm able to do this shit because I got two nuts and a dick. It's not a woman's place to be in the streets wildin'. If I die, it's because I was out handling my business. If she die, it's because her ass was runnin' loose in the streets doin' dumb shit because she in her feelings."

"Correct me if I'm wrong, tho'. It sounds like you the one in yo' feelings. You talkin' like you give a fuck if she lives or die," I told him.

"Nah, that's where you wrong, I don't give a fuck. I'm just a nigga lookin' at it as a nigga should. Dropping straight facts," he answered with a shoulder shrug.

"Man, whatever."

Hamin could speak that macho man shit to the next nigga all day long, but I knew that nigga better than anyone. He was feeling little mama, and that nigga was dealing with a bruised ego because the chick he wanted was chasing a dead nigga in the grave. This was exactly why I stayed away from this love shit, and he was completely violating by falling for the fucking connect. I just hoped that when this shit was all said and done that they could separate the two, because if not, we were fucked.

CHAPTER SIXTEEN

Empriss

The tension between me and Hamin was out of this world. The bullshit with Jose happened almost two months ago and he was still giving me the cold shoulder. For his last two pickups, he would send Ace to deal with me and to make sure that shit was in order, and he would either stay outside of the warehouse or he would stand there looking at his phone, smiling like he had just won the lottery.

They had another pickup coming up in a few days, and I wasn't ready to deal with the bullshit. Even though I had only known Hamin a short amount of time, in that short time, I admired him and the man that he was. Hamin was different from any other distributor I had. Him and Ace were something I had never seen before. It made me think back to the question I asked Javier when he had first brought Hamin to my attention.

He told me that I had to make sacrifices when the situation would be beneficial to me and back then, I didn't understand why he felt that Hamin could benefit me, but now I could. He moved more keys than the other two distributors combined, and what first started out as 120 soon turned in to 150, and I had got word that they wanted to move up the weight again. I wasn't sure how they were getting them off so fast, but if we were getting money together, I could ignore all the hostility between us. Money would always be the motive.

Throwing my legs over the side of the bed, a wave a nausea swept over me. Bolting to the bathroom, I made it to the toilet just in time before everything I had ate for dinner the night before came up.

Dammit, I knew those fuckin' lobster tails tasted funny, I thought, wiping the side of my mouth.

Brushing my teeth, I started to feel worse as the seconds ticked by. All I wanted to do was lay in the bed and sleep my life away. Once I was done, I headed down to the kitchen to see if we had anything for nausea.

"Good morning, Lulu. Do we have anything for an upset stomach? I don't know what I ate, but it's not agreeing with my stomach," I told her, brushing my bushy hair out of my face.

"Oh no, you too? Little Jaiyce woke up this morning throwing up and he says he has a stomachache. I was coming down to find him some ginger ale and crackers to see if that would help," she said.

"I think it was the lobster tails that you fixed last night. Let me go check on him."

"That would explain why I'm not sick. I didn't eat any but I did take some home to my husband. I know he will be calling me soon. You go get back in the bed and I will bring you up something to help your stomach."

"I can do it, Lulu. I still need to go out later. I have a meeting with

Papa, and you know how he feels about being late."

"Mr. Ortis will just have to understand. Now go. In bed, Empriss. I will be there in a minute," Lulu said, shooing me out of the kitchen.

"I'm going, I'm going. I'll be in JJ's room."

On my way to JJ's room, I swore I heard him talking to someone, but after I didn't hear anything, I assumed it was the TV and knocked on the door.

"Come in," he called out.

"Hey, big man. Lulu said you weren't feeling good," I told him, making my way into the room.

"My stomach hurts."

"Mine does too. How about we lay in bed and watch cartoons all day?" I asked, scooting the bed beside him.

"But it's Sunday. You have to go to Papa's today," he told me.

"I think Papa will understand if I miss one day with him. Besides, I think we deserve a lazy day just you and me, don't you think?"

Nodding his head eagerly at me, he broke into the toothless smile I loved so much.

"Yeah, I think we do. Can we watch *How to Train Your Dragon* and *Big Hero 6*?"

"We can watch anything you want to, baby," I answered, pushing his curls out of his face. "Go put the movie in."

"Okay, Mama," he answered, excited, bouncing off the bed and over to his TV stand.

Watching JJ, my mind started to wander back to the pictures that I had seen of his father when he was a baby. He was the spitting image of him, and it hurt me that he would never know what it was like to have a father. Feeling the tears well up in my eyes, I wiped them before he could see them.

"Mama, can I ask you something?" JJ asked, easing back in the bed.

"Sure, baby. What is it?"

"Is Ha mad at me?" he asked, catching me by surprise.

"No, baby. Why would he be mad at you?"

"Well, I thought he was my friend, but he hasn't been by to see me. I thought I did something to make him mad at me and not be my friend anymore."

"Oh, baby, no. Hamin is still your friend. He's just mad at mommy right now," I told him, sitting up in the bed.

"Can you make him not mad at you anymore so he will come see me? I want to play futbol with him again. I know you don't like him, but he's nice to me and he plays with me," he said, breaking my heart.

"Okay, baby. I'll fix it," I told him, pulling him close to my chest.

I wasn't the only one affected by Hamin's absence, and JJ just made me realize how stupid I was. I would do anything to see a smile on my baby's face, even if that meant I had to suck up my pride and apologize to Hamin.

* * * *

Pacing the warehouse floor, I tried to calm my breathing and keep my palms from sweating, but it seemed like the more I tried, the antsier I became. This was supposed to be a normal meeting the same way we did every month, but I knew this time was different.

Tires connecting with the gravel outside had my heart attempting to break free from my chest. Wiping my hands on my pants, I straightened my back and waited for Hamin and Ace to step out of the car.

"What's up, Em? How you feelin', Esteban. Luke," Ace greeted, stepping into the warehouse.

Giving Ace the once over, I had to admit to myself that he was a good-looking man. He was six feet two, deep chocolate, pearly white teeth, and baby boy's body was banging. When I say his melanin was popping, I mean that shit. His nose ring and beard just pushed him over the edge, even with all that, I still only had eyes for Hamin.

"Hey, Ace. How was the flight?" I asked.

"It was straight. You know a nigga be tired as fuck afterwards."

"Yeah, I know." I laughed. "Hey, Hamin."

"Oh, what's up," he answered flatly before looking back on down at his phone.

Ace must have felt the tension because he cleared his throat and clapped his hands together.

"Look, y'all makin' this shit weird as fuck, and I ain't beat, mane. I'on know what the fuck y'all gotta do but this shit right here ain't workin' no more," Ace said, gesturing between the two of us.

"Mane, I'm good. That's all shorty. We makin' money together and everybody eatin', so we good," Hamin replied, sliding his phone in his pocket. "You good?" He asked, giving me his undivided attention.

"Umm," I started, clearing my throat. "Yeah, I'm good."

"See. Everybody good. Esteban. Luke. Let's get this shit together and this money counted so we can hop back on this red eye and I can get these crates put away."

"Wait, you're not staying?" I asked with a little more panic in my voice than I wanted to show.

"Nah. I gotta make it back to Memphis by the mornin'. I got shit to handle," he answered, looking at me sideways.

"Oh, okay. JJ asked about you," I blurted out, making him stop in his tracks. "He'd like to see you. I'm sure he'd understand if you had to leave."

"I'll stop by and see the little nigga before we head out," he said over his shoulders.

He agreed to see JJ and that was all I truly cared about, but I knew that he wasn't dealing with me at all. If that's how it was going to be then so be it, I would suck it up and handle this shit like the boss I was. Hamin wanted to act as if I wasn't shit, then okay, we could do that. But I bet that I played the game better.

CHAPTER SEVENTEEN

Hamin

"What's wrong, lil' man?" I asked JJ, sitting next to him on the back steps.

"Why haven't you been by to see me?" he questioned.

"I just been busy. I've been back in Memphis handling a lot of business there. Opening up the little men's club and all that."

"I thought you weren't my friend anymore. I was scared mama scared you off."

"Ya mama couldn't scare me away if she wanted to." I laughed. "You don't worry about what's going on between me and yo mama. We will handle things if it's meant to be handled."

"I think mama likes you," he told me, smiling.

"Boy, ya mama don't like nobody."

"She likes you though. I can tell."

"You can tell, huh? Well I can't. But enough about that. We gon' play this game of soccer or what?"

"It's futbol," he corrected while laughing.

115

"Soccer. Futbol. Kickball. Whatever you wanna call it. You ready to play or what?" I joked.

"Yep. I'ma beat you so bad."

"Show me what you got then."

We played in the yard until well after dark. JJ reminded me why a nigga was ready to settle down and start a family. I wasn't getting any younger, and to be honest, I wouldn't mind having that life with Empriss, but I could tell it was wishful thinking. Empriss was too caught up in her past to see her future standing in front of her, and I wasn't the nigga to try to prove anything to her. She'd be alright.

I ended up staying way longer than I expected. JJ cried when I was getting ready to bounce, so I decided to stick around. I ate dinner with him, helped him get ready for bed, and even laid on the couch and watched TV with him until he finally fell asleep.

Laying him down in his bed, I pulled the covers back and tucked him in. Hitting the lights, the stars stuck to the ceiling, lighting up his room with enough light. Giving him one last look, I pulled the door up and made my way to the living room to grab my shoes so that I could leave.

"Hamin, can I talk to you for a minute?" Empriss asked, stepping into the living room.

"Speak, shorty. This ya house, I can't stop you from doin' what you wanna do in ya shit," I told her, lacing up my shoes.

"I'm sorry," she said.

Bringing my eyes up to look at her, I leaned back and just stared at her for a minute. She looked nervous as hell, bouncing from foot to foot, and kept wringing her hands together.

"For what?"

"For everything. I wasn't trying to make you feel any kind of way."

"But that don't explain why you apologizing to me. Why apologize for somethin' that you wanted to do? Like you pointed out to me, I ain't ya nigga or ya daddy. I was just a nigga layin' dick," I told her honestly, shrugging my shoulders.

I had gave up on the idea that Empriss would ever give a fuck about anybody but herself and JJ. Hell, that's what she's supposed to do. In the words of Rihanna, I was just another nigga on the hit list. Shorty didn't owe me shit.

"But look, I'm out. Same time next month. I'm out."

"Ha, wait! You don't understand."

"What is there to understand? Why is it important to make me understand? Quit beatin' around the bush, mane, and just tell me what it is. I got a flight to catch," I told her, not hiding my attitude.

She saying a nigga don't understand, but she ain't painting a clear picture either. What was I supposed to be understanding?

"He was all I had."

"Who was all you had?" I asked, confused.

"Jaiyce! He was all I had and they took him from me. They stole the only person to ever mean something to me in this world away. They are the reason I'm afraid to love. I'm afraid that if I get too happy, someone would come and snatch them away from me too. The day I walked out of that prison, I made two promises to myself: I vowed to kill them off one by one until this hole they created was filled, and that I would never love another man again."

"Man, I ain't got time for this shit. I'm not about to sit here while you tell me why you in love wit' the next nigga. I get it, ma, you out for revenge and you wanna make them motherfuckas pay. If that's what you wanna do, shorty, then be my guest. If I said it once, I'll say it again, YOU DON'T OWE ME SHIT!"

"That's what you not understanding. I do owe it to you to explain because you're the only person that I've ever let myself feel for besides Javier and Jaiyce. I try to fight it, but I care, Hamin. I care what you think about… what you think about me. You don't make me feel like Empriss, you make me feel like me again. The real me," she explained, casting her eyes to the floor.

"The real you?"

Now shorty was starting to confuse a nigga, for real. Out of nowhere, I got this strange feeling in the pit of my stomach that I didn't want to finish this conversation; that whatever she was about to say to me would change shit for me. "And there's something else," she started, dropping her head in to her hands. "I'm pregnant."

Mane, fuck!

Ain't this about a bitch.

CHAPTER EIGHTEEN

Empriss

Keeping my face buried in my hands, I waited for Hamin's reaction to my news. I had been feeling funny ever since I got over my food poisoning. I don't know what possessed me to take the pregnancy test, but I did, and when it read pregnant, everything changed for me. I already had one child that I was trying to parent all while juggling being America's Most Wanted, but to bring a newborn in to this was something completely different altogether.

Realizing that he still hadn't said anything, I slowly lifted my head to find him staring at me with this blank expression on his face.

"Did you hear me?"

"Uh. Yeah. You sure?" he questioned, clearing his throat.

"I only took one test. I haven't made an appointment yet or anything, but I don't think I want to have the baby," I admitted.

"What?"

"Let's be real, Hamin. Bringing a baby into this isn't going to help anything. I'm already trying to juggle JJ. I can't have a baby to worry about too. The unknown scares me on a daily. Like, what if the people that killed Jaiyce came back and snatched JJ to get to me? What if the enemies that I've created over the years come and take them away from me? I would never be able to live with myself if anything happened to them because of my past."

"Shut up wit' that bullshit, Empriss. I hate to break it to you, but the moment you let them words fly out ya mouth that you was pregnant, that no longer became ya decision. If you wanted to get an abortion, you should've just kept that shit to ya self and prayed that I never found out."

"But—"

"We are not discussing this shit! You not killin' my baby!" he yelled. The look on his face was so menacing, and the malice in his voice made me jump back in my seat a little.

"So, what you're saying is it's fuck what I think and what I want? I have no opinion?"

"Shorty, you always got an opinion. It's ya body, and at the end of the day, you do what you think is best. You got ya opinion and I got mine. Just know that if you kill my seed, we ain't got shit else to talk about. No amount of money in the world can make me keep dealin' witcha. I'll just have to find another way to get my money. Kill my baby and you dead to me, and that's on Allah," he said, walking out the room.

Sinking to the floor, I let my head fall back on the ottoman and watched the fan spin. This conversation went completely different in my head when I came to stop him. I pictured myself pouring my heart out to him and then telling him I was pregnant, and we ended up having freaky sex and he would tell me he wanted me to be his girl. Boy, was I wrong.

Getting myself up off the floor, I made my way upstairs to get in my bed, I was ready to just crawl in my bed and forget the conversation that just took place. I wanted so bad to tell Hamin my real name and who I truly was, but seeing his reaction to me saying I wanted an abortion made me glad that I changed my mind at the last minute.

Something was telling me that he wouldn't understand, or care for that matter. I know that I had to tell him one day and very soon, but not tonight. It was a conversation for another day, and I was dreading when that day actually came.

* * * *

Pregnancy wasn't very becoming of me; between morning sickness, having to pee every sixty seconds, and my mood swings, I could live without this shit. Hamin had been on my back constantly about making a doctor's appointment, and I had been coming up with excuse after excuse of why I hadn't made it yet. I thought that I could keep him at bay for a little while longer, but this asshole took it upon himself to call the doctor's office to make my appointment himself.

I was starting to show and I knew that I couldn't keep hiding behind my big shirts or dodging Javier. I wasn't sure how he would take the news, but in the back of my mind, I knew he wouldn't be mad. The way he kept pushing Hamin off on me, he wouldn't be surprised one bit that I ended up pregnant.

Dressing down in an olive maxi skirt and cream colored tank

top, I sprayed my body down in my Thousand Wishes body spray from Bath & Body Works before slipping my feet into my nude wedges. Standing to my feet, I smoothed out my outfit and gave myself a once over in the mirror.

"Aye, you ready to go?" Hamin asked, barging into the hotel room.

We had flown out to Little Havana late last night for my doctor's appointment with my OB/GYN. I loved Cuba, but I definitely wanted my baby to be a US citizen, and I had been seeing Sabrina for all these years, so it was only right that she delivered this baby too. But I was still trying to figure out how Hamin found her all the way down here in Miami. Sneaky bastard.

"Uh, yeah. I just need to grab my purse," I told him, stepping around the bed to grab my wristlet off the small table.

"What the fuck is them on your feet? You need to take them off before you fall and hurt the baby or some shit."

"What's wrong with my shoes?" I asked, looking down at my wedges. They weren't even that high, so I didn't see why he was tripping so hard.

"You pregnant, Empriss, you don't need to be wearin' heels. Who the fuck you tryin' to look good for anyway?"

"There is nothing wrong with my shoes, Hamin, and besides, it's not like I'm walking around in stilettos," I said, rolling my eyes in my head. "C'mon, or we're goin' to be late."

"We ain't goin' nowhere until you change them damn shoes."

I had to stare at his face to see if he was serious and he was. There wasn't a trace of humor on his face. I watched him sit down on the edge of the bed and get comfortable.

"Are you serious?"

"Very."

Blowing out a frustrated breath, I plopped down on the bed beside him and snatched the shoes off my feet, before sliding my feet into the gold thong sandals I wore on the plane ride over here. They didn't even match my outfit.

"You happy now?"

"Yep. Now let's go," he said, getting up off the bed and heading out of the hotel room.

"Punk ass," I whispered, sucking my teeth.

The ride over to the doctor wasn't long at all. We were there in less than ten minutes. All of a sudden, this feeling washed over me and I became extremely anxious. Wringing my hands together, I wiped my palms on my skirt and got out the car.

"You aight?" Ha asked, giving me a strange look as we walked up the sidewalk towards the door.

Looking over at him, I simply nodded my head, too afraid to speak thinking my voice would get the best of me.

Stepping in the lobby, it wasn't as packed as it normally was. There was only one other couple and a lady sitting by herself that looked to be ready to pop any day now. Walking up to the counter, I smiled at Holly, the receptionist.

"Hey, girl. What are you doing here? You don't have another appointment until three months from now, if I'm not mistaken," she said, looking over at her computer to double check to make sure she was right.

"Uh, yeah. My boyfriend called and made me an appointment."

"Yeah, I called earlier this week and scheduled an appointment with Sabrina Rochester. The appointment is at 1:15," Hamin told her.

"Ummm, I'm sorry, but the appointment I have here is for an Em..." she started to say but stopped mid-sentence when I started to cough uncontrollably.

"Damn. You good, mane?" Hamin asked, patting me on the back.

"I think I need some water. Can you grab me some?" I asked, gesturing towards the water machine across the room.

"Yeah, I'll be right back."

"Thanks," I said, waiting for him to walk away before turning around to face Holly. "That appointment is mine. Could you please just put it down as Empriss, please, Holly? I'll explain later," I whispered just as Hamin walked back up.

"Sure. You're all set. The nurse will call you back in just a minute," she told me.

"Thank you."

Sitting down in my seat, I couldn't stop my leg from bouncing, and I realized I hadn't thought this situation through at all. My chest felt like it was tightening and I didn't have asthma. Taking a sip of my water, I tried to calm my nerves when I saw Hamin throwing glances my way every few seconds.

"Empriss Reed," the nurse called.

Standing to my feet, she gave me a strange look and I knew she was about to ask, but I gestured for her not to say anything by pressing my fingers to my lips. Kicking myself, I should have just quit being a punk and made my own appointment, but no, Mr. Inspector Gadget had to find a way to locate my damn doctor, and now I was about to get caught up, and that scared me more than being on the run.

"Get undressed from the waist down and the doctor will be in with you in just a minute," the nurse said after she ran all my vitals and took a urine sample from me.

Doing as I was told, I laid back on the small table and said a silent prayer to God that he saw me through this appointment. Five minutes later, I heard the room door open and my heart dropped in my feet. It was like time stood still.

"Hi. I'm doctor Rochester, but you can call me Sabrina," she said, greeting Hamin.

"You must be my new patient?" she asked. Dropping my arm down that was covering my face, I sat up and faced her. "Oh, hi, Rebekah. They said that I had a new patient here by the name of Empriss Reed. They must have gotten the appointment times mixed up," she said, sliding on her gloves. "You're back earlier than planned. What can I do for you today?" she asked, facing me.

I could feel Hamin's eyes boring in to the side of my face and I couldn't look at him even if I wanted to. I was terrified of what I would see.

"I'm pregnant," I told her once I finally found my voice.

"I saw that there was a positive pregnancy test in the chart. Congratulations. When was the last day of your last period?"

"I think it was the 23rd of April."

"Hmmm… so that would put you roughly around four months. So you should be about sixteen weeks, give or take."

"Mm hmm," I answered, still never looking over at Hamin.

After asking me a few more questions, she told me that she was sending the ultrasound technician in to check on the baby since I had gone four months without any type of prenatal care, and to give me my estimated due date. The moment the door closed behind her, time stood still and I waited for Hamin to start bombarding me with questions, but to my surprise, he stayed silent.

Letting my eyes finally turn to lock with his, I saw his face showed no emotion. I couldn't tell what he was thinking and I think that scared me more than anything.

"Ha—" I started but the door opening cut me off.

"Hi. I'm Leah. I'm the ultrasound tech. First, let me say congratulations to you both on your pregnancy," she said, smiling, setting up her equipment. "Now this is going to be a little cold," she warned, before pouring this cool blue gel on my small baby bump. "If we're lucky, we may be able to tell what you're having, but it's still a little early so let's not get our hopes up."

The moment the wand connected with my baby, I could feel Hamin approach the table closest to my head and place his hand on my shoulder.

"Yo, what's that?" he asked, pointing at the screen with his free hand.

"That is the baby's arms. And here are the legs and the spine," she replied, pointing out everything as she spoke. "Let's see if we can hear the baby's heartbeat," she said, pressing the wand down a little into my stomach before clicking some buttons on her keyboard.

The moment the sound came on and I heard the weird little sound come in to the room, I swear it was one of the most precious noises I had heard in my life, other than JJ's laugh.

"Why it sounds like that?"

"Fetus heartbeats are a little more erratic and they beat a little more rapid than a full-grown baby or adult. They beat around 120 to 160 beats per minute, and it slowly decreases during gestation as the due date nears."

"Oh, aight. I'on know what none of that shit mean, but if you do, then we good," he said, causing her to laugh.

"I'm not completely 100% sure, but I'd say about 80% sure that I can tell what you're having. Would you like to know?" she asked, looking between me and Hamin.

"Hell yeah," he blurted before I could even get anything out.

Instead of the tech telling us out loud what the baby was, she typed it on the screen and printed out the few pictures she'd taken of the baby. Reaching the pictures out, Hamin snatched them up and went on the other side of the room to look at them. I watched him as he looked at the pictures with a smile plastered across his face.

"Well?" I urged sitting up.

"I'll see you in the car," he said, the smiling dropping from his face before he walked out the room letting the door slam shut behind him.

I should have known that shit would have gone downhill after the happy moment was over. Taking a deep breath, I slipped my skirt back on and smoothed my hand down over my stomach, just as the baby kicked.

"Yeah. Your daddy's gonna be the death of me; wish me luck," I said out loud, rubbing my bump before walking out the room.

Here goes nothing.

CHAPTER NINETEEN

Hamin

Rebekah? What were the fucking odds that her name was Rebekah? I kept trying to tell myself that she wasn't the chick that Khalid was looking for, but in the back of my mind, I knew that no matter how much I hoped and prayed, she was her.

Stepping out in to the air, I paced on the sidewalk, running my hand down my face. Staring down at the ultrasound in my hands, I smirked as the reality that I would be someone's father soon kept replaying in my head. I would do everything in my power to never let any harm come to my baby, meaning that I had to protect my baby mama, even if that meant with my life.

Letting my head fall back, I looked up at the sky to say a quick prayer, asking Allah to get me through this. I wasn't sure how I was going to make it, but I knew that I had to try. I just didn't know how I would trust Empriss, Rebekah, or whatever the fuck her name was after this. This whole situation was giving a nigga a migraine out of this world, and a nigga wasn't pressed at all for this shit.

"Are you mad at me?" Empriss had the nerve to ask, stepping up behind me.

"Mane, shut the fuck up talkin' to me," I sneered, making my way to the car where Luke was waiting on us.

"Hamin. Let me explain," she said right before I grabbed the handle. Letting my hand fall from the door, I spun around on my heels and walked back to where she was standing, mugging the shit out of her.

"Explain? Explain what, ma? What is there to fuckin' explain? That you a fuckin' liar!" I chuckled angrily, trying my hardest to keep my hands to myself.

The fucked up part about all this shit was that I cared about Empriss and JJ. I looked at him as if he were my son, in a sense. The lil' nigga was like my best friend or some shit.

"How do you tell someone the most important thing in the world and you know they would never believe you?" she asked in a low voice.

"I'd try, Empriss, damn!"

"But I knew you'd act like this," she tried to explain.

"You don't know how the fuck I would have reacted if you had just gave me a fuckin' chance by tellin' me yourself instead of me having to find out like this. Do you know how the fuck it feels to find out that yo' baby mama ain't even who the fuck you think she is? What else you hidin' from me, huh? What, you actually did kill ya baby daddy or was that Rebekah?" I snapped.

"That's not fair."

"Newsflash, shorty, life ain't fair. Get in the car; we'll talk about this shit later," I told her, storming off.

"But, Hamin—"

"Empriss, get in the fuckin' car! We'll take about this shit later!" I yelled, causing her to jump back a little with tears in her eyes before walking towards the car.

Running my hand down my face, I tried to keep my attitude at bay because I knew shit was about to get more hectic by the second, but before I took on this bullshit ass task at hand, I needed to make sure she deserved it. What the fuck had I gotten myself into?

Getting in the back seat, I stared out the window as Luke drove us back to the hotel. Miami was a beautiful city and I couldn't even focus on sightseeing because all this shit kept repeatedly playing in my head.

"Were you ever gone tell me?" I heard myself ask, not even bothering to look in her direction.

"No," she whispered, and that was all I needed to hear.

My phone chiming in my pocket. I pulled it out and unlocked the screen to see I had a text from Khalid.

What were the fuckin' odds, I thought as I clicked the icon to open the message.

Khalid: Any word on her?

Me: Nah. I got some people lookin' in to it tho.

Khalid: Cool. Make sure you get up with me when you get back around so we can figure this shit out.

Me: Ight.

Sliding my phone back in my pocket, I looked up just in time to see we were pulling back up in front of the hotel. Thinking about something, I grabbed my phone back out of my pocket and sent another text message.

Me: Look in to houses out here in Miami. We about to set up shop.

Ace: Miami? Why nigga?

Me: I'll be home in a week and we'll talk then. Just do what I said nigga

Ace: Motherfucka, please is a fuckin' word.

Me: Lol nigga fuck you.

Ace: I ain't no faggot for one and two, this dick too grade A to be wastin' on niggas. I ain't no fuckin' booty bandit. Get off my line for I change my damn mind and shit.

Me: As salaamu Alakium

Ace: Wa Alaikumu Salaam

Chuckling, I shook my head as the wheels in my head started spinning. Miami would be a good look, but Memphis was a nigga home, but I knew I couldn't spend the next few months in Cuba, so that meant that I needed to be somewhere close enough to drive and not have to hop on a plane every other week. No one was looking at me now, but I knew it was only a matter of time before the police started snooping around. I wasn't wishing bad on myself; a nigga was thinking realistically, so I needed to make smart moves when I could. Feeling Empriss's eyes on me, I looked up to see her staring at me with a scowl on her face.

"What?" I asked staring back at her.

"Nothing," she said, scoffing before getting out the car and slamming the door behind her.

Shorty was gon' be the death of me, I could feel it. All I know is we had a long ass eighteen years ahead of us, so we better get on the same page or shit was gone only get worse.

* * * *

"It's been three days, are you really still not talkin' to me?" Empriss asked walking in to the kitchen.

Starting at her feet, I let my eyes roam over her body. I couldn't lie, she looked good enough to eat. I admired her smooth chocolate skin and the small pink silk robe she had on. Letting my eyes fall against her baby bump, I finally brought them to her lips and then finally her face. Watching her bite on her bottom lip, my dick jumped in my boxers as I thought about the feel of her lips gliding up and down my dick. It had been a minute since my dick touched any part of her body, and a nigga would be lying if I said I didn't miss it.

"You don't hear me talkin' to you?" she asked again once I didn't answer her.

Leaving my facial expression blank, I just stared at her before setting my fork down beside my plate and leaning back in the barstool.

"What you want from me, shorty?" I finally asked.

"What do you mean what I want from you? You haven't talked to me since the day in Miami, and we been back in Cuba for the past two days and you haven't looked at me. Not once."

"Just because you don't see me lookin', doesn't mean I don't."

"That's not what I mean, Hamin, and you know it." She sighed.

"You better be glad that I'm even here right now. I should've left yo' ass in Miami and took my ass back to Memphis, but instead, I came here to watch out for you."

"And to make matters worse, you still won't show me the ultrasound pictures. You even showed JJ, and he refuses to tell me anything because he says I'm on punishment." She pouted.

Call me petty or harsh, but I hadn't told her anything about the sex of the baby, and until she talked to me without trying to get one over on me, then she was stuck. If I was willing to put my neck on the line for shorty, I needed her to do the same thing and at least be honest with a nigga.

"You knew that I would find out eventually. Why not just tell me yourself when you found out that you were pregnant?"

"I wanted to, I swear I did, but I just couldn't."

"You gotta do better than that, shorty. Why not?"

"Because."

"Because what, Empriss? Just spit that shit out. It ain't rocket science. WHY DIDN'T YOU TELL ME!"

"BECAUSE I DIDN'T TRUST YOU, OKAY?" she yelled. "I couldn't trust you. Half the time, I didn't even know if I wanted to like you. I wanted to hate you most days, I tried to convince myself that I did hate you. I thought that if you knew the truth, you would try to kill me just like the rest. Like you told me the day we got in to it, you can get your coke from anywhere, so killin' me wouldn't be shit to you."

"You think that the past six months have just been for fun for me? You think a nigga go around kissing ass and fuckin' all my connects? Quit playing with me like my life ain't real."

"And do you think hiding the true me from people I get close to is easy for me? I wanted to tell you because you make me feel like the old me, the real me, and I show you her. You are the only one I have ever let get close enough to open up the true me. Not this fucked up ass persona that I have learned to be, but the person I was before Jaiyce was murdered and my life changed. That was the sign that I got too close to you. That's why I had to stay away from you and my true feelings for you. I can't be Rebekah; I have no choice but to be Empriss. She's who I am now. A part of me died the day I walked in my apartment and saw him with a bullet to his head, covered in blood. It was bad enough that they came back to finish me, but then I ended up in jail three months pregnant on a twenty-five to life charge, and my only choice was to either serve the time for something I didn't do or be this. The choice was easy. I just never thought I would have to be myself again, then I met you," she told me, leaning on the counter beside me and dropping her head.

Studying the side of her face, I softened up when I realized she was telling the truth. Something about her tone let me know that she meant every word that she said. Reaching out, I pulled her into my lap and made her face me.

"Look at me for a second, shorty," I demanded in a low tone. When her eyes met mine and I searched them and found what I was looking for, I grabbed her hand and laid it across my chest. "I can only do as much as you allow a nigga to, and I'm not with the lying bullshit, so this shit stops now. Everything needs to be laid out now. No holdin' back because if I find out you lied to me again or you holdin' out secrets, shit gon' get real ugly, real fast. I'on like to repeat myself, shorty, and I damn sure ain't tryin' to look like no duck when all I'm tryin' to do is be there for you. I ain't sayin' I love you or no shit like that, but a nigga rockin' wit' you and I'd do anything for you and lil' man. Especially our baby girl. I can only be ya nigga if you let me. I ride for you, you ride for me. I shoot for you, you better bust back for me. I know we got this shit goin' on wit' this business shit and trust, I'll always let you handle that street shit, but when we home, I'm the king of this castle. I can be ya worker all day, every day, and that nigga that's goin' to war for you, but to be real witchu, I'd rather be ya nigga, you gon' let me?" I asked, looking in to her eyes so that she knew I meant every word.

I'm not a sucka by far and I'on wanna believe that Empriss would try to play me as one, but I could see it in her eyes that she wanted a nigga to love her, and I'd be damned if I wasn't gon' be the main man in my kids' lives. JJ was mine off the strength, and we had a daughter on the way. I could let Empriss continue this queen pin shit, but I needed her to understand that if she agreed to be mine, that I was the king.

"It's a girl?" she asked, smiling down at me hard as hell. Shorty was showing all thirty-two.

"Yep. Now answer my question, but before you do, understand this. Ain't no more runnin' after a ghost and tryin' to be the next Angelina Jolie when she was on Mr. & Mrs. Smith, while you pregnant with my daughter, Empriss. I'm not tellin' you that I want you to quit this street shit completely because you was doin' this shit way before a nigga ever saw ya face, but no killin' motherfuckas and no handling business alone. We clear?"

"Okay, babe. I got you," she answered looking at me.

A part of me felt like she was lying, but I would give her the benefit of the doubt and try this trust thing with her because I felt like shorty was put in my path for a reason. I just hoped that this shit stayed on the up and up, but the dreams were steady coming and I could feel shit was about to hit the fan soon. I just hoped I was prepared for the shit before they came after Empriss. Khalid and his uncle were determined to get they hands on her, and I knew they wouldn't stop because I was "having trouble" finding her. They would be coming for her sooner rather than later and I planned to have that red dot waiting. I was who I was for a reason. They'd better ask about me.

CHAPTER TWENTY

Khalid

"What do you mean, you still can't find her? How hard could it be to find some little black bitch from Memphis?" my uncle's voice boomed from the other side of my headset.

"Hell, you ain't been able to find her either, and you supposed to be a mob boss, the fuck you mean?" I said before I could catch myself.

"What the fuck did you just say to me?" he asked, his accent seeping through.

"I'm just sayin', Unc, you know for yourself that this shit ain't as easy as it seems. The bitch is like a fuckin' ghost. We ain't even got an up-to-date picture of her, but I got someone lookin' into it for me."

"Listen to me, and hear me good. If she finds us before we find her, it's a wrap for all this we've built, and I won't lose my empire because of some little cunt with a vengeance."

"I hear you, Unc. But let me hit you back, someone else is on my line," I said.

"Don't you—" he started to say before I hung up the phone in his ear.

I wasn't trying to hear nothing else this nigga had to say. Granted, I owed my life to my uncle and I meant that shit literally. If it wasn't for him, who knows where the fuck I would be. He raised me after my pimpin' ass pops killed my mama and then turned around and killed himself when the police raided their spot. He was one of them possessive ass niggas on some if *I can't have you then no one can* type of shit. It was basically fuck me and how I would survive, but fuck it.

Racking my brain, I started to think of how to get to this Rebekah bitch. My uncle had been searching for her for a hot minute, and to be honest with you, I was trying to figure out how much damage one bitch could do; but he was sure that if she found us before we found her, then shit was a wrap and our lives would be turned upside down. So I was trusting him because he had never given me a reason to doubt him and his judgement.

Snatching my keys off my office desk, I headed out to get some answers. I still wasn't able to keep in touch with Hamin for more than a couple days out the week, and every conversation that we had, he was telling me that he was still following up on leads, and I knew that was bullshit.

One thing anyone knew when it came to Hamin Shakespeare was that the nigga was good at what he did. There was no such thing as a dead end when it came to him. This nigga could have found Osama bin Laden had Obama asked him to, so either this bitch was as good at hiding as they say, or we were looking in the wrong place.

Hitting the locks on my brand-new Audi truck, I hit the automatic start button and threw it in drive, burning rubber all the way down the block. I was on a mission. I needed to see a man about a dog and I knew that one way or another, I was going to find this bitch; and if Hamin was having trouble finding her, then I was about to give this nigga a little push.

It took me about thirty minutes to make it to the Southside of Memphis, and I hopped out my truck, scanning my surrounds until my eyes landed on who I was looking for. I spotted Ace sitting on an AC unit behind one of the apartment building directly across from the basketball court. Swaggering over to where he was, all eyes were on me, niggas was sizing me up left and right, and bitches were smiling trying to be seen.

Nothing about me was ugly at all, and because I was a pretty boy, motherfuckas thought I was soft, but I loved when motherfuckas underestimated me; it made their fall that much harder. I stood six feet two and was a good 230. Hoes loved the fact that a nigga was bowlegged, but between my waves, green eyes, thick lips and goatee, I wasn't sure which had them feening for me more. Yeah, ya boy was fine and I knew it.

"Ayo, Ace, let me holla at you for a minute," I called out once I was in arm's length of him.

"Whatever you gotta say, you better spit that shit out. I know you see I'm in the middle of somethin'," he said, sucking his teeth and giving me the once over.

"Why you always act like you got a problem wit' me when you see me?"

"Who said I was actin'? Mane, speak yo' peace on why you came in my hood witcha chest poked all out. I ain't wit' that back and forth shit. I'll leave that to you and the rest of the bitches that walk this hood. Now what you want?" he snapped, taking his eyes away from the game he was watching unfold on the basketball court to look at me with the permanent scowl that he always wore.

No man pumped fear in my heart, but I was smart enough to choose my battles, and in the middle of South Memphis solo wasn't the right place to check this nigga, but my trigger finger was itching to lay this nigga out.

See, Ace had this reputation around the hood after he snatched a nigga's mama for owing him some money from a dice game. When I say the nigga was ducking and dodging Ace at every corner, you would have thought that he owed the man his life, but come to find out, he snatched that man over a hundred dollars. What kind of motherfucka snatches someone mama over a hundred dollars? Apparently, this nigga. When ol' boy came around the hood with the money to get his moms back, Ace made that man strip butt ass naked in the street and pistol whipped him and told him to keep the money; it was more so about the principle than anything, and homeboy violated when he tried to get over on him.

"You and Hamin owe me somethin', and I came here to collect," I told him, stuffing my hands in my pockets.

"Owe you? Nigga, let's be clear on somethin'. I'on owe no man shit. I pay all my debts when I collect them, and seeing as how I ain't got shit from you, that mean I'on owe you a motherfuckin' thing. I'ma tell you like this, whatever Ha agreed to do for you ain't got shit to do wit' me. You better call that man."

"Nigga, you got a lot of mouth, you know that shit, right? It's time someone fixed that shit for you, fam," I sneered, pulling out my pistol and aiming it in his direction. When I did, every nigga that was around pulled out and cocked whatever banger they had on them.

If it was my time to die, then so be it, but I was tired of these niggas treating me like I was deer meat or some shit.

"Oh, so you tough, huh?" Ace mocked.

"I'on know, nigga, you ready to find out?" I snarled.

"Shit, hell yeah," he said jumping off the AC unit, walking toward me and putting the gun directly in his chest. "What's up, nigga? What you tryna do?"

Squeezing the trigger, my pistol clicked and I realized that my safety was still on it. The laugh that erupted from Ace's chest had me looking at this nigga like he was a got damn psychopath.

"Oh shit, you was ready to smoke a nigga? You just earned a little respect from a nigga." He laughed, going back to his spot on the AC like I still didn't have my gun drawn. "What Ha was supposed to be doin' for you?"

"He was lookin' into findin' this bitch named Rebekah for me, but he said he keep comin' up empty handed, and I'on know if I believe that," I said, sticking my gun back in the small of my back.

"If he said he comin' up short then I believe him, but I'll talk to him about it."

"Aight. That's all I'm askin'," I told him, turning around, getting ready to leave.

"Khalid, if you ever in yo' life pull a gun out on me, I'ma send three straight through ya fuckin' head like a bowling ball, then I'ma hunt down every person you've ever called ya snake ass lovin' and doin' the same shit. All the way down to ya neighbor's dog. I fuck wit' you off the strength of Ha, don't forget that shit," Ace said to my back.

I didn't have to look at his face to tell he was dead ass serious. Instead of answering, I hit the nigga with the deuces and went on about my business. I had accomplished what I had come here to do and as long as he was gone talk to Hamin, then we didn't have shit else to talk about until they came up with an answer or a body to give me, but even still, I was gon' do my own research.

Jumping back behind the wheel of my truck, I brought it to life and threw it in drive.

"Siri, call Ques," I commanded, pulling away from the apartment complex.

"Yo," he answered after the second ring.

"Aye, you remember that chick Rebekah that I been lookin' into for my uncle?"

"Yeah, what about her?" he asked.

"I need you to pull all her school records and find her parents. Looks like I'ma have to do this shit myself."

"Say no more. Gimme a week and I'll hit you back with somethin'," he said, and I could hear him clicking away on his keyboard.

"Bet. Don't let me down, nigga," I said, ending the phone call.

Shit, if Hamin wanted to pussyfoot around the situation then I would take matters in my own hands, but either way it went, Rebekah's days were slowly coming to an end, and I didn't give a fuck if I had to follow shorty to the end of the Earth. Her day was coming and I planned to be the nigga to take her out of here.

Sending out a few texts on my phone through voice command, I made sure that everyone was on standby at all times because I could feel that shit was about to get rocky and soon; and on the real, I welcomed that shit with open arms. The sooner the better. Shit, ready or not, Rebekah, here I come.

CHAPTER TWENTY-ONE

Ace

As soon as I watched Khalid's bitch ass pull out the parking lot, I pulled out my phone and called Hamin. I didn't like the fact that Khalid came searching for me. Even though I wasn't hard to find, shit had me feeling some type of way.

"What's wrong?" he answered after the third ring.

"How you know somethin' wrong, mane?" I laughed.

"The only time you call me these days is if some bullshit done popped off, so what is it?"

"Ya boy came over to the Southside lookin' for the kid," I told him, looking over my shoulder towards the basketball game. I had fifty riding on the skins to win and I wasn't in the art of losing money. I'd fuck around and shoot all them niggas.

"My boy?"

"Yep. Khalid lil' punk ass. Lil' nigga pulled a gun out on me and shit," I told him, chuckling.

"He what?" His voice boomed and I could tell by his tone this nigga was ready for war already, and he hadn't even heard the whole story yet. That's why he was my nigga.

"Calm down. Shit wasn't even that deep. He rolled around the hood, we had words. I guess the nigga felt played so he pulled his gun out. Pussy pulled the trigga too, but forgot it was on safety. Fuckin' dumbass. Anyway, he said some shit about he came to collect information that we owed him. Something about some bitch you supposed to be findin' named Rebekah."

The way this nigga breathed in the phone let me know right off the bat that whatever he was about to say wasn't about to be good.

"Mane, that shit complicated. I need you to make it down here in the next few days. Meet me in Miami though when I link up with this realtor about these houses."

"What the fuck have you gotten us in to? You know a nigga ready to bust them thangs at any given time with no questions asked, but you gotta give me a lil' more than 'it's complicated,'" I told him.

"We'll talk about it when you get down here. Meet me in Miami in a couple of days. Look, I gotta go. Be on time, Ace. Shit 'bout to get real and I need to make sure that you up for this shit."

"Don't insult me, my nigga. I'll be there."

"Aight bet. Assalamu Aalaikum."

"Wa alaikumus salaam," I returned before hanging up the phone.

Between me and Hamin, we stayed in some bullshit, which meant we were always bringing each other into our shit. Like that nigga Kevin Hart said, my bullshit was his bullshit and his bullshit was my bullshit.

This what the fuck we signed up for, but I knew Hamin. If he said shit was complicated than that means it was. Either way it went, I was headed to Miami, the land of naked bitches and mistakes. Hell yeah, I was down for whatever. Call me Quagmire 'cause I was ready to give them broads this gigidy, ya dig?

* * * *

Three days later...

I get Celine for my bitch that do the postal

I get that brick, I get that bird from coast to coastal

I hit the papi then them bitches screamin', "Ayyyy"

I mix then pump my wrist and whip 'til it's dry

I threw that dope and all that dodi in the bushes

I heard the feds was lookin' for me, got to book it

I know you're sellin' but you need to cut the price

I get that pack and run that bitch like Jerry Rice

I came through the subdivision thumpin' "Woods" by Tory Lanez through my speakers. When I first heard his music, I thought he was one of them singing ass niggas, but when I heard this song, I had to give him his props 'cause he was bumping.

Some white lady was standing outside watering her flowers was looking at me like I had three heads, so when I hopped out the car shirtless, I hit her ass with a wink and a 100-watt smile, and just like I knew she would, she started blushing.

I knew I was these bitches' dream; white or black, young or old, they were feeling the kid regardless. Swaggering up the driveway, I had to admit I was feeling this house. It had two stories with a long ass driveway, and from the front, you could tell that it had a big ass backyard.

Walking through the foyer, I looked around and that bitch was laid out. The walkway had me ready to buy it and I hadn't even seen the rest of the house yet.

"Mane, you heavy, ain't it?" I said to Hamin once I found him in the kitchen standing next to this Jessica Rabbit lookalike.

"Hell yeah," he said, smiling, slapping up with me. "I'm feeling this shit, for real, for real."

"You must be Mr....?" she started reaching her hand out to shake mine.

"Ace," I told her, giving her the once over. Shorty had this whole naughty school teacher thing going on, with the black pencil skirt, white button up, and red bottoms. Most of her fire-red hair was pulled up into one of them messy buns females loved so much, but her bang was swooped down over her eye with her glasses barely poking out from behind it.

"Mr. Ace. I'm Jessica Sanders," she greeted me, causing me to laugh.

"Name fits you perfect 'cause I was just thinkin' you looked like my favorite character, Jessica Rabbit," I told her honestly, not trying to hide the fact that I was eye fucking her.

"I get that a lot. I take it that you like this house?"

"Yeah, this shit nice. I'ma need somethin' just like it, but a lil' more dope. Think you can handle that?"

"I'm sure I can handle whatever task you put in front of me." She began flirting, running her tongue over her lips. "I actually have a four-bedroom house three doors down that I think will be perfect for you. Want to go look at it with me?"

"Yeah. Gimme about an hour. Go grab lunch or somethin' and let me and my boy handle business. I'll have Ha hit you when I'm ready," I told her.

"Okay. You two have a good rest of the day. Mr. Shakespeare, I left the paperwork on the counter," she said before strutting off toward the front of the house. Once I heard the door open and close, I turned my full attention to Ha and waited for him to open his lips and let some words spill out.

"You gon' tell me what's goin' on or I'ma have to beg you to open up ya lips?"

"Empriss is pregnant," he said with a smile across his face.

"Oh shit! Congratulations then, my nigga. Now that that's out the way, tell me what's goin' on with this Khalid bullshit. You made it sound like the world was about to fall apart when you heard he came to the hood."

I watched him as the smile dropped from his face and stress took over it. He rubbed his hand down his face before bringing his eyes up to look at my face like he had the weight of the world on his shoulders.

"Mane, listen. Before I tell you what's goin' on, I need you to understand that I'm not askin' you to take on this shit wit' me. If you hear what this shit is then decide you don't want no parts, then all I can do is respect it. This shit bigger than Memphis beef. This shit on a whole new level of fucked up wit' some enemies we don't want to have," he explained.

"Just spit the shit out, my nigga. You'll never know unless you ask me."

"About six years ago, the prince of the cartel got murdered in his house back in Memphis. Apparently, it was some retaliation type shit. Anyway, the shit was bad, they put one through the back of ol' boy head, killed his grandma and hunted down his moms and everything. The chick that was supposed to be responsible for the shit was this Rebekah chick, which was his girlfriend at the time.

She went down for his murder and everything. She got convicted and was sentenced to serve 25 to life. All evidence led to her. Fingerprints on the gun and everything. Three weeks after she was sentenced, she disappeared from her cell—"

"What you mean she disappeared from her cell?" I asked, interrupting him.

"What I just said, shorty disappeared like poof, gone, vanished into thin air and no one's seen lil' mama since."

"Okay, so what's the problem?" I questioned not understanding.

"I found her," he told me.

"Then hand the bitch over and we can go on about our business. This shit ain't got nothin' to do wit' us."

"That's where you wrong, it has everything to do wit' us," he said, pausing. "The Rebekah chick is Empriss," he admitted, instantly making my head hurt.

"Wait, what? Run that by me one more time."

"You heard me right the first time. Empriss is the chick they lookin' for."

"Ha, what the fuck? You protecting this bitch and for what, 'cause you put a baby in her? Shit, you can get plenty more of those. She murdered the cartel prince and you want to go to war with them over that? C'mon my nigga, the pussy can't be that good," I snapped, getting up out my seat and pacing the floor.

"She didn't do it, mane. I'on know why or what she knows, but they set her up. I don't know who murdered that nigga but I got to find out why before my daughter get pulled into this shit. If I believed she did it and I ain't give a fuck about her, then I'd hand her over to Khalid and his people's wit' no problem, but she tellin' the truth, man. She didn't kill that nigga."

"You willing to bet yo' life on that?" I asked, looking at him.

"I already have," he answered with no hesitation.

"I hope you know what the fuck you done got us in to. This broad pussy better cure cancer and AIDS for all the trouble you goin' through. What's the plan?"

"That means you in?"

"Do rabbits fuck like it's goin' out of style? Hell yeah, I'm in, you shouldn't even have to ask. We need to figure out how the fuck Khalid and his people wrapped up in this shit too, because why would he be wanting to look for her so bad unless he got somethin' to do wit' that nigga death."

"I was thinkin' the same shit. I'on know how, but he knows more than he's lettin' on, but I plan to get to the bottom of this shit. I got five months before my baby girl make her appearance on this Earth, so that means I got five months to wrap this shit up or at least get close to doing so. I don't need no unnecessary bullshit at my doorstep. My baby mama already a fuckin' fugitive, I sell more dope than a little bit, and my best friend a certified sociopath. That shit enough by itself," he said, shaking his head.

"Nigga, I ain't no fuckin' sociopath. I just like killin' niggas," I told him, shrugging my shoulders.

"Yo' ass cuckoo for coco puffs is what the fuck you is."

"But bitches love me though, so I'm good." I laughed. "Now that we got this out the way, I got two things on my agenda for the rest of the week. I'm about to go see if Jessica can hit them notes like Jessica Rabbit, and slide up in some of this wet Miami pussy. I'm in the land of freaks and I'm tryin' to hit booty clubs and show off this monster at one of these naked beaches, ya feel me?"

"Nigga, pussy all you think about?"

"Nah, I think about money and killin' stupid people too."

"You a fool," he joked.

"But I was so serious," I admitted with a straight face. Money, pussy, and murder was all that I thought about. At least I could admit that shit to myself. I was a fucked up individual and I had my reasons to be, and I was okay with that.

"I know you were. But let me get out of here. I got Empriss ass up in a hotel and she keep blowin' me up about bringing her greedy ass something to eat."

"Aight. Hit me later so we can make something shake and I'ma get in touch wit' some people to see if I can find out more about Khalid and who his peoples is," I told him, dapping him up.

"Aight," he said, and with that, he was gone.

I knew there was a reason that I didn't like Khalid's bitch ass, and now that I knew he was wrapped up in some funny shit, this gave me the only reason I needed to hit his ass with that double tap. Sending out a 911 text message to my homeboy that me and Ha worked with from time to time I let him know I was in need of his services. If anyone can find the info I needed, it would be him.

I would wait for him to hit me back and depending on what he said, I would handle the situation accordingly. In the meantime, though, it was time to go jump in some pussy. I needed all I could get before my life got hectic, and I knew that shit would be soon, so I was about to enjoy myself.

CHAPTER TWENTY-TWO

Khalid

*P*ulling up to the address that Ques had sent me over, I double checked it to make sure that I was in the right place. It took him a little over a week to find the information I was looking for. Checking the clip on my pistol, I made sure it was full before sticking it in my waistband.

Taking in my surroundings, I had to admit that it was pretty nice and secluded over here; from what I heard about its occupants, they had a rough background. Making my way up the steps, I rung the doorbell and waited for someone to answer the door.

"Can I help you?" a big tall burly looking dude asked answering the door.

"Yes. I was looking for the parents of Rebekah Stevens," I told him, plastering a fake smile on my face.

"You know Rebekah?" a small chocolate woman questioned, coming into view from behind the door.

"We went to school together. I've been away for a while and when I came back around, I wanted to find her."

"Well, if you know Rebekah then you know that we didn't raise her. We lost her to the system when she was two years old, and when she got older, she didn't want anything to do with us. So, if you'd please excuse us," the man said, getting ready to close the door in my face.

"Curtis. Stop it. Come on in, baby," the woman said, hitting his arm and stepping to the side for me to enter.

"Thank you."

"How long have you know Rebekah?" she asked, sitting down on the couch.

"Um, since about ninth grade. From what I hear, she disappeared off the face of the Earth. I just wanted to catch up with her and talk to her about a few things," I lied, looking around the living room.

"Well, if you and Rebekah were such good friends, then you would have known she was in foster care, would you not?" Curtis inquired, testing my patience.

"You're right, but I went by her old foster mother's house and she no longer stays there, so this was my next best bet. Just because she didn't stay with you guys, doesn't mean she didn't know your names. You're not that hard to find ya know?" I told him, a threat in my tone that I was praying he caught.

His time was coming a lot sooner than he thought. I was beyond ready to knock this nigga off.

"Humph," he grumbled before stepping out of the room.

"Please excuse my husband. Rebekah is a sore subject for us. We were on drugs pretty bad when she was born and to be honest with you, I'm surprised CPS didn't come sooner than what they did. We tried reaching out to her when she started junior high, but she didn't want anything to do with us," she said with sadness in her voice.

"Do you know if her for foster mother would have a way to get in touch with her?" I asked, putting my hand on her shoulder, attempting to console her.

"I'm sure she does. They were close, and Rebekah loved that woman like she was her biological mother. Let me see if I can get the address and phone number for you."

"Okay, great. Do you mind if I use your bathroom for a second?"

"Sure. Down the hall, third door on your right."

"Thank you."

Making my way down the hall, I slid my biker gloves on my hands before I made it to the bathroom door. Locking the door behind me, I took the silencer out of my pocket and screwed it on to my gun. Easing the door open, I tiptoed to the room where I heard the TV playing, and eased up behind Curtis and put two in his head before he even realized I was in the room.

Making my way back towards the living room, I saw her mother leaned over the counter scribbling something on a piece of paper.

"Hey, is that for me?" I asked making my presence known.

"Yes, baby. Here is the number and address," she said, turning around, only to be met with two slugs to the chest.

The shock in her eyes made me feel a little bad, but I couldn't risk them telling anyone that I came around here looking for Rebekah.

Rather them than me. Picking up the piece of paper from the floor where she dropped it, I backtracked and made sure that I wiped my fingerprints off the coffee table and door where I touched it, and just like that, I was gone as fast as I'd come.

Jogging down to my truck, I pulled out my phone and dialed Ques's phone number and waited for him to answer.

"Yeah?"

"Aye, send the clean-up crew over to Rebekah's parents' house and I'm about to send you the address to her foster mom's crib. Send Rocko and Trip over there to handle that. Get as much info out of her as possible. If they gotta kill the bitch then do it, but either way it goes, send two through her. No witnesses, and I can't risk no loose ends. We clear?"

"Yeah, we clear."

"Good. I need to hear something by the end of the night," I told him, hanging up the phone in his ear.

I could feel the trail to Rebekah getting warmer and warmer, and I knew that if anyone could point me in the right direction, then it would be her foster lady. I needed to figure it out and fast though. My uncle's patience was wearing thin and I didn't need them type of problems in my life. One thing for sure though and two things for certain, if it came down to it, I'd knock that nigga off. Uncle or not, he could get this issue. Fuck he thought?

* * * *

Around a quarter to midnight, my phone started blowing up left and right with calls and texts from Rocko, Ques, and a couple from my uncle.

Deciding to hit Ques back first, I put the phone on speaker and waited for him to answer.

"It's done. She wouldn't talk so Rocko burned the house down with her in it."

"He didn't get nothing?"

"I didn't say that. Apparently, her and Rebekah still do keep in touch. We didn't find any pictures of her anywhere, but there were some pictures of her and a little boy over the past few years. From him being born to birthday parties and even soccer games. We even found the hospital he was born in. I'ma send you everything over."

"What I'ma do with info on a little boy?" I asked more to myself than him.

"I'on know, but just a head's up. Your uncle reached out to me and Rocko. I'on think he too happy that you been doing shit without him okayin' it. Think you might want to hit that nigga up ASAP."

"Alright. Good lookin' out, mane."

Ending the call, I sat back and got my thoughts together before dialing my uncle's number. For as long as I could remember, he was always two steps ahead of me. If I made any kind of moves, he was right there looking over my shoulder to make sure I did what I was supposed to do.

"Why wasn't I aware that you decided to look up the little bitch's parents?" he asked, voice booming and his accent shining through.

"I was waiting until I made sure that the leads worked out before telling you."

"So, what did you find out?"

"That she has a son and if I can get to him, I can get to her. I have Ques bringing me over the pictures and the information about his birth."

"You better not fuck this up, Khalid. I already had to make sure that your lil' minions did their job the right way when it came to disposing of her foster mother. What if it got back to her that we were looking for her or if she had gotten a hold of the tapes from the security cameras?"

"What security cameras?" I asked.

"If you don't think that Rebekah would put security cameras outside of her place, then you're dumber than I thought you were. I want this situation handled and fast. We're runnin' out of time," he said, hanging up the phone in my ear.

Looking down at my phone, I blew out a breath of frustration and just as I was putting my phone down, a text came through.

Ques: *Check your fax.*

Walking to my home office, I picked up everything he sent over. Staring at the pictures of the little boy, something stuck out about him but I couldn't figure out what it was. Deciding not to dwell on it, I pushed the thoughts to the back of my head. Dropping the pictures in my desk drawer, I put them there for safe keeping. I would get Hamin to handle that when he made it back in town. Shit, it was the least he could do now that he botched the other side of it. If I couldn't get Rebekah to come out of whatever hole she'd crawled in to, then I knew snatching her son would have her coming to me. Let the games begin.

CHAPTER TWENTY-THREE

Empriss

Two months later…

My relationship with Hamin had been one of bliss, especially since we moved out to Little Havana. I still had to run things in Cuba and he still had to go back to Memphis a couple times a month, but for the most part, we were in each other's presence.

I had caught him sneak whispering on his phone in the middle of the night and I wouldn't say insecurity, but I would be lying if I said I didn't think it was another woman every now and then. I wasn't sure if the pregnancy and extra weight gain had me feeling self-conscious, but I didn't like the feeling one bit.

Glancing over at the clock on Hamin's side of the bed, I noticed that it was a little after seven in the morning, so I eased out of the bed, careful not to wake him up. Grabbing my burner cell on the way out, I tiptoed to the adjoining bathroom and dialed the number I called at least three times a day.

The call immediately went to voicemail, and the same feeling I had been getting over the past couple of months washed over me. Something had to be wrong with Mama Jo. We talked at least once a week and this was going on the second month not talking to her. We had little gaps here and there because she understood that I couldn't always talk like that, but whenever I called, she answered.

Last time we talked, I told her about the baby and she was so excited, her and JJ sat on the phone for fifteen minutes trying to come up with baby names, all of which Hamin shot down. He said he didn't like any of them.

Hitting the speed dial number on my actual cell, I waited for Luke to answer.

"Is there somethin' wrong Ms. Reed?" he asked immediately.

"I'm not sure. Do me a favor and send Esteban and Carlos to Memphis to check on mama. She hasn't been answering her phone and I'm starting to get worried. Check on her and tell them to call me immediately," I told him.

"Yes, ma'am. Do you want them to check in about the other thing too?" he asked, catching me off guard.

"Yes, but we won't talk about that over the phone. I'll get that information when I get back home."

"Yes, ma'am."

Once the call ended, I stared at the wall while I chewed on my bottom lip. I know I promised Hamin that I would let the situation with Jaiyce go, and I had been doing good for a while now, but a part of me just couldn't let go until I knew the truth. I just had to make sure that Ha never found out because if he knew I was still searching for the people responsible, he would stop dealing with me indefinitely and I couldn't let that happen. Him, JJ and Harmony were my life.

"What are you doin' in here?" Hamin asked, causing me to jump out of my skin.

"Sorry, baby. Luke called and I didn't want to wake you, so I got out of the bed to answer," I answered, standing to my feet and waddling over to where he stood.

Standing on my tiptoes, I leaned up to kiss on his lips. Bringing his bottom lip in to my mouth, I sucked on it a little before letting go.

"You better stop. That's how you got that one." He laughed, poking me in the stomach.

"I know, but you're so sexy when you first wake up in the morning. Especially since your beard is all scruffy," I said, tugging on his thick beard.

I wasn't lying though. Hamin had always been sexy to me, but now that I was pregnant, just the sight of him alone could make my pussy wet. It was like no matter how much we made love, I couldn't get enough of him.

"Gone now, Empriss, before you wake him up. I'm about to get back in the bed and get these last two hours of sleep before I catch my flight. Come get in the bed with me," he said scooping me up in to his arms and carrying me to the bed bridal style.

When he laid me down, he hovered his body on top of mine,

careful not to lay his weight on top of me or my stomach.

"You're gorgeous, you know that?" he asked, looking down in my eyes.

"Quit looking at me like that."

"I can't help it. You really are gorgeous, shorty. You gon' be the death of a nigga, I swear."

"Ride or die, right?"

"Right," he answered, crashing his lips in to mine.

Wrapping my arms around his neck, I deepened the kiss and started to run my fingers through his hair, only to have him to break the kiss and pull out of my grasp.

"You know the rules, ma. You gotta take what you want," he taunted, laying back on the bed and placing his hands behind his head.

Biting on my bottom lip, I eyed the tent in his boxers and my mouth immediately started to water. Unleashing my favorite toy, I licked my lips before going to work on it.

Slurping, licking, nibbling and humming in a pattern, I felt the spit gather up in the back of my throat before letting it seep down the sides and on to his dick. Looking up at him, I watched his internal battle as he tried hard not to let the feeling of my mouth take over him.

"Ssssssss, fuck, Em," he hissed, closing his eyes tight.

Using that as motivation, I started to bob my head up and down like my life depended on it. I don't know if it was just me, but there was something about hearing the man you love moan out in pleasure because of you. I swear it was the sexiest noise on this Earth.

"Come bring me that pussy," he demanded in a low voice, eyes heavy with lust.

Doing as I was told, I slid my panties to the side and eased down on him, moaning as I tried to adjust to his size.

"Uh-huh, take that dick."

"Ahhhhh!" I cried out, my head falling back.

The sound of our skin colliding against one another, our heavy breathing mixed with our moans was driving me completely insane.

"Spin around and let me watch it," Hamin groaned placing his hands on my hips to keep me in on his dick as I spun around.

Leaning forward, I grabbed on to his ankles, careful not to hit my stomach as I bounced up and down on him like a pogo stick.

"Ssssss… just like that."

"Dammit it, Ha. I'm about to cummmm!" I screamed out a little too loud.

Bringing his body up, he pressed his chest to my back bringing his right hand around to lightly grab the sides of my neck applying just enough pressure to send me over the edge. My walls started to grip on to his dick for dear life as an orgasm started to rack my body.

Picking up his pace, he applied a little more pressure to my neck before sinking his teeth in my shoulder and I swear that was all she wrote.

"HAMINNNNNNNNN!" I screamed as the orgasm took over my body, causing me to go limp.

"Fuckkkk, Empriss. Shit!" he moaned out, exploding right behind me.

Panting, I let my body lay against his until he laid back on the bed with me still in his arms.

"This shit right here is dangerous as hell," he panted.

"But is it worth it?" I asked, eyes still closed.

"Of course," he answered, kissing the back of my hair. "Empriss, you know I love you, right?" he asked as sleep tried to take over my body.

"You what?"

"I said I love you. I would never let anything happen to you, JJ, or baby girl. Y'all are my life and I'd die protectin' y'all. If shit get rough, I need you to know that," he said, causing me to roll over and look at him.

"Where'd that come from?"

There was something about his tone that I didn't like. I was happy that he finally confessed his love for me even though I never really needed him to say it. I kind of just always knew, but now that he was telling me, it was like he was trying to explain it to me without telling me the whole story. Like there was more to it.

"It came from my heart. Just listen to a nigga for a second. I know I don't say it but I do love you. I just need you to trust me and let me be the man for once. Without all that extra shit."

"I love you too, Hamin."

"I know you do, shorty," he said before kissing me on the forehead and wrapping his arms around me.

That feeling that I got earlier was slowly creeping back into my heart, but this time I couldn't shake it. Something was wrong, and even though it hadn't hit yet, I could feel that it was about to. That things were about to get knocked off balance. Things were too quiet. Just a little too perfect. I didn't want to be superstitious, but I was one of those people that believed that if things were perfect for too long that tragedy was soon to follow.

I just prayed that whatever it was, we would be strong enough to deal with it together and that my hunt for Jaiyce's killers wouldn't come back to bite me in the ass. I just needed a little more time, and I prayed that God gave it to me but even as I drifted off to sleep, I could tell it was wishful thinking.

* * * *

Stepping off the plane, I made my way over to where Luke and Esteban were parked waiting on me. Between the plane ride and these red bottoms I had on, all I wanted to do was lay it down, but I knew that I couldn't. I had business to handle, so sleep would just have to wait.

The drive to my villa was short so I didn't have to wait long before hearing what information the boys had gathered for me. A part of me was a nervous wreck for more reasons than one. I was worried about Mama Jo because I still wasn't able to get in touch with her.

"What did you find out for me?" I asked, taking a seat behind my office desk, looking over some of the papers that littered it.

When they didn't say anything, it caused me to look up, and that's when I finally noticed the sad expressions on their faces.

"What's wrong?"

"We went to the house but it was completely burned down to the ground. The neighbors said that there was some type of electrical fire and that Mama Jo got trapped inside. I'm sorry, Ms. Reed. She's gone," Esteban said, hanging his head.

"Gone? What do you mean gone?" I barely recognized my own voice from the amount of pain that was in it.

I can honestly say that I haven't felt this type of hurt in over six years, and I honestly never thought that I would feel this way again any time soon.

The scream that came out of my chest and up through my throat scared me on so many levels that if I didn't see my mouth open through the mirror that was across the room, I wouldn't have believed it was me.

No one would ever understand my relationship with Mama Jo. She had been there for me when the rest of the world gave up on me. I gave her some hard times when I was a teen coming in to my own and learning what it meant to be a parentless child, but between her and Jaiyce, they kept me on the straight and narrow and I became one of the students in high school with the top GPA's because of the love and guidance that they showed me.

When I got sent to prison, it rattled her to the core and she dropped sick for a while. She was at every court date and she would have been there to visit me had I not put her on my refusal list. I just knew in my heart that I was going to have my son in prison. The thought of never being able to raise him or meet him for that matter was too much to bear. When I miraculously got out of prison, Mama didn't ask any questions. I believe she already knew what it meant. She just asked that I keep in touch with her as often as I could, and over the years I had done that. I had kept my end of the deal and now, I had lost two of the people that meant the world to me.

"Ma'am, there's something else," Luke said, clearing his throat. "The neighbor said they found this in their mailbox the day after it happened. It didn't have a return address or anything, just your name sketched across the front."

Reaching out to grab the manila envelope that he was extending to me, I looked at my name across the front of it and my whole life stood still. Drying the tears from my eyes, I broke the seal with shaky hands and looked inside, only to find a piece of paper and some type of tape.

Without acknowledging the letter, I handed Luke the tape so that I could see what was on it. Pressing play, there was completely darkness for a second before the picture finally came into view. Cramps immediately shot through my stomach as I watched the TV screen in horror.

"I'm goin' to ask you one more time, old lady? Where can I find Rebekah?" the masked man demanded, crouching down in front of her so that they were eye level.

She was bound to a chair, and from what I could see, her face was battered and bruised up like they had been torturing her for hours.

"I don't know who you're talking about," she answered stubbornly.

"Lady, on everything I love, I don't mind killing old people. You

willin' to die for a bitch that's not even here to protect you?"

"If it's my time to die, so be it."

I watched in horror as he grabbed the canteen and doused her body in gasoline, making sure that he got the curtains and couches good. There seemed to be a knock or something in the background that distracted him. Pulling out his gun, he disappeared off camera for a few minutes before returning with a well-dressed gentleman.

"What are you doing here? Lid didn't say anything 'bout you comin'?" the masked man asked.

"Because he doesn't know," was his only reply. *"Go around the house. Grab all the pictures you can find of anyone close to her and search her bedroom for any lead on Rebekah,"* he commanded, never taking his eyes away from Mama.

When the masked man disappeared to do what he was told, the man in the suit took a step closer to her, and the look of apparent fear in her eyes instantly angered me.

"Is she worth losin' your life over?" he asked. *"You can make all this go away if you just tell me where I can find her."*

"Please, just tell him," I pleaded in a low voice. I knew she couldn't hear me and that she was already gone, but I wanted to save her.

"Why are you doing this to us? You of all people? What has she ever done to you?" she asked angrily.

Stepping closer to her, he leaned down and whispered something in her ear, and the look of confusion, shock, and hurt that flashed through her eyes didn't go unnoticed. Dropping her head, she began to cry, and not knowing what he said to make her cry did something to me. I became undone. All the tears that I had stopped from flowing came back full force and with a vengeance, as everything on the screen began to move in slow motion.

All of a sudden, Mama Jo lifted her head and looked directly at the position of the cameras I had installed in her house. She smiled and began to quote the Lord's Prayer.

"It's okay, baby. This isn't your fault. I love you," she spoke.

"Who are you talking to?" the man asked, lifting his head up to look at the camera.

I could tell the video had been distorted because the man's face was immediately blurred out.

"To answer your question, she is worth it," she told him.

I watched as the masked man entered the room with a backpack full of stuff that he grabbed from around the house. Pulling out a gun that had a silencer on the end of it, he shot Mama Jo once between the eyes and twice in the heart to make sure that she was dead.

"Clean this up," the man in the suit instructed before walking out the door.

The masked man struck a match and tossed it at her feet before walking out of the living room, as flames engulfed it and the camera cut off.

Remembering the letter that was in the envelope, I unfolded it to see what it said. Opening the letter, the only thing written on it was an address and five words.

You can find him here.

I wasn't sure exactly who he was, and I know I promised Hamin that I would stay as far away from this as possible, but they forced my hand. This is why I said Rebekah died a long time ago. She was a shy and timid girl that only wanted to be accepted and loved; but Empriss, she was a whole different breed. Her heart was vengeful and she didn't care who she had to kill to protect hers.

"Don't tell Hamin about this. Burn the tape and the letter. This meeting never happened," I told Luke and Esteban getting up from my chair.

"But, Ms. Reed…" Luke started to say, but the look of death I gave him stopped whatever words were getting ready to make their way out of his throat. "Yes, ma'am," he finally agreed, before walking out of the room with Esteban following close behind him.

Hearing the door close behind them, I broke down and allowed my body to slide to the ground. Feeling Harmony kick, I placed my hand on my stomach.

"I will never let anyone harm you or your brother," I vowed.

I don't know how long I sat in that spot crying, but once I was done, all the crying and sadness was out of my system, and hatred and blood thirst replaced it. They wanted to find Rebekah so bad, I would make it easy for them. I was the predator and they were officially the prey.

"Come out, come out wherever you are. You can run, but you won't get far," I whispered repeatedly to myself. "Ready or not, here I come."

CHAPTER TWENTY-FOUR

Hamin

Three weeks later...

*M*ost days a nigga didn't know whether he was coming or going. Between stepping up and moving more dope for Empriss, I had taken over the drug game, in not only Tennessee, but I became the main supplier in South Beach and Virginia. Once Javier found out that Empriss was pregnant, he started to show me more and more on the Cuban cartel so that I could run things in Empriss's place while she was on maternity leave, or eventually take over for her completely.

To be real, the dream was only to stack money and get the fuck on with my life, but I would be lying if I said being the boss of a cartel wouldn't be the shit. That was more Empriss's forte though. I was cool being the nigga on the streets instead of the man behind the chair.

Thinking about Empriss, I had noticed over the past few weeks, she had been moodier than normal. It seemed like she was always on edge and any time a nigga said anything, she acted like she was ready to bite my fucking head off; and when she didn't have an attitude or was being a bitch, she was crying every two seconds. I had asked her doctor about it and she said that mood swings were normal in the third trimester because the body was going through so many changes so quickly, but I didn't know how much more of this shit I could take.

Baby girl was due in a month and a half and I was nowhere near clearing this shit up with Khalid and his people. Between me and Ace, we had gotten a few answers but everywhere we turned, it was like the trail ran cold. On the real, it was like Khalid surfaced out of thin air. Like one day the nigga just fell on the streets of Memphis. The nigga came with clout off the strength. No working his way to the top or nothing, the nigga was just here.

To add the icing on top of the cake, that nigga had been blowing me up a lot more than usual, making Empriss give me the side eye. When I say every time my phone rung and I got up to go answer it in the next room, baby girl's eyes were on me like a fucking hawk. The shit was intimidating and sexy as fuck all at the same time.

He kept saying that next time I touched down in Memphis he needed to see me, and since I needed to link up with Ace and the crew again before Harmony made her appearance, then I would go ahead and link up with him. Shit, I was ready to just cut all the bullshit out and put two in that nigga's dome off the strength and call it a day.

"Baby?" Empriss called out, stepping into my man cave.

"What's up?" I asked, looking over to where she stood in the doorway.

When I say Empriss was the most beautiful thing on this Earth to a nigga, I wasn't even fronting. I couldn't even put it into words what being in shorty's presence did to a nigga. Like I'd get all nervous and my heart would start beating out of my chest.

"When do you leave?"

"I leave out tomorrow morning. I got some things to wrap up here with Javier before I leave, then I should be home by Friday night. Come here, what's wrong?"

"Just sad that you're going to miss my last ultrasound appointment." She pouted, sitting down in my lap.

"You know how many pictures we got of that little girl already and she ain't even made it here yet. Trust me, baby, she knows daddy loves her and that I will be one of the first faces she sees when she graces us wit' her presence," I told her, rubbing her stomach, feeling Harmony kick my hand. "See, she agrees wit' me," I joked.

"Ohh," she groaned in pain. "I will be so happy when this is over with. I just want my body back."

"You ain't got much longer. You'll survive, pimp." I laughed, tapping her on the ass.

"You say that because it isn't your body that's being bent all out of shape," she complained, smacking her teeth.

"Yeah, yeah, whatever. You hungry?"

"Yesssss."

"I don't even know why I asked. Hop up for a minute and I'll go whip you up some food in the kitchen, and we'll spend the rest of the day doin' whatever it is you wanna do, witcha crybaby ass."

"I am not a crybaby," she whined, causing me to laugh harder at the distraught face she was making.

"Mane, get off my lap so I can go cook or yo' big ass gone starve," I joked.

When I say shorty shot up off my lap with a quickness, I kid you not. That's the fastest I'd seen her ass move in months, but she was out of my lap and across the room in 2.5 seconds flat. Big mama didn't play when it came to food or anything food related.

"Fat ass!" I yelled.

"I love you too!" she yelled back.

Making my way down to the kitchen, I whipped up some cheese eggs, grits, turkey bacon, french toast, and a fruit salad. After I was finished, I called her and JJ to come down for breakfast.

"Oh shit, a nigga right on time," I heard Ace say, walking in to the kitchen.

"Nigga, do you believe in knockin'?"

"Hell nah. What I'm knockin' for when yo' ass don't never lock the slide door in the first place. That shit would be dumb on my part," he answered, smacking his teeth before heading over to the sink to wash his hands.

"Well good morning to you too, Ace," Empriss said, waddling in to the kitchen.

"What's up, big mama?" he joked. "What's up lil' mama?" he said, rubbing her stomach before grabbing a plate off the counter. "Yo' ass look uncomfortable as fuck. You sure you only seven months?"

"Fuck you, Ace!"

"What? It ain't my fault ya ass over there lookin' like you giving birth to a toddler. You gone be like that pregnant giraffe I been seeing all down my damn timeline."

"April still hasn't had that baby?" Empriss asked, taking a bite of her bacon.

"Hell nah. She probably was lying to her baby daddy about when she got pregnant and now the pressure on. See how y'all females do? Even the animals be lying, tryin' to trap niggas. Damn shame," Ace said, shaking his head.

"I'm convinced you were dropped on your head as a child," I told him, laughing.

"It's the truth, hell. These females be trappin' niggas. He better get a DNA test when that giraffe finally comes into the world. It probably ain't even his."

I couldn't do shit but laugh because I could tell this nigga was dead ass serious. I swear this nigga didn't have all his marbles.

"Uncle Aceee!" JJ yelled, coming down the stairs full speed.

"What's crankin', lil' nigga? You been workin' on yo' dribbling like I told you to?" Aced asked him, lifting him to sit on the barstool beside him.

"What did I tell you and Hamin about callin' my baby a nigga?" Empriss said.

"Leave that man alone, Em. He ain't hurtin' nothing. You act like we do the shit to purposely be disrespectful or some shit," I told her, fixing my plate.

"It's okay, Mama. I don't mind," JJ said smiling.

"And you just don't see me, huh?" I asked, throwing a piece of bacon at JJ.

"I'm sorry, Ha. Good morning," he said, jumping down from his spot and coming to hug my legs.

"I thought so," I joked, lifting him into my arms.

"Put him down, Hamin."

"Woman, if you don't sit yo' ass over there and eat that food and leave us alone. Tell ya mama she always buggin'. We over here vibin' and shit."

"Yeah, mama, you buggin'. We over here vibin' and shit," JJ told her.

"JJ!" Empriss yelled, leaning over the counter to hit him.

"You better not hit him. Don't say shit tho', JJ. Understand?" I asked, looking at him.

"Yes, sir," he answered nodding his head.

"That's why he my nigga," Ace joked.

We couldn't do shit but fall out laughing as Empriss shook her head at us. He was gon' be hell when he was coming up, but I wouldn't have it any other way. I didn't want him to be like me, I wanted him to be a better man than me, and I would show him how to be just that.

For the rest of the morning, we sat around laughing and just enjoying each other's company. I wouldn't trade them for anything in the world and I would do everything I could to protect them.

* * * *

"What is it that you wanted to talk to me about?" Javier asked once I opened the door for him.

I had sent for Javier a couple of days ago because I knew I couldn't make the trip to Cuba and make it back home in the time frame I set for myself.

"I'm headed back to Memphis for a few days, but if I don't come back, I need you to continue to watch out for Empriss, JJ, and Harmony for me," I told him, stepping to the side for him to enter, and taking a seat on the couch.

"I thought you were only goin' to town to look over your operation?" he questioned, sitting in the chair across from me.

"I am, but I also have some loose ends that I need to tie up. These loose ends don't just affect me tho'. They determinantal to all of us, but I can handle it," I explained.

"Then why do you need me to step up in your place if you don't come back?" he asked, causing me to stop and think for a second.

"Because I can't predict the future. I don't know what's goin' to happen from the time I hop in that car and drive away, to when I make it to Memphis and handle my business. I just need to know that my family is taken care of if I leave this place and don't come back."

"That's one of the things I admire about you, Hamin; you always put the ones you love before yourself. I was taking care of Empriss and JJ long before you knew they existed, and it would only be right that I look out for them long after you're gone. As long as there is air in my lungs, they will never want for anything, and I will protect them with my life as I always have. Even little Harmony," he told me, lifting the weight that I had on my shoulders.

"That's all I ask," I told him.

"I have never seen Empriss love anyone the way she loves you. I can only imagine the love she had for my son because I wasn't around to witness it, and I know I seem to be hard on her, but it's only because I want what's best for her, and you are that. You can protect her in ways that I can't because we don't view her the same. A man will do anything in this world for his child, but the strength that drives a man that's in love with a woman, the mother of his child at that, is something completely different.

There isn't a force strong enough to stop that man. Not when he understands what he has to lose, and you are that man. Empriss is lucky to have you, and even though I wish my son were here to be in their lives, I know for a fact that it was written that you be the man in her life. The man to turn her in to the beautiful woman and mother that she is blossoming into every day."

"Thank you. I love Empriss, and no one can tell me that JJ isn't my son. I love that little boy like I went half on him myself. Just watch over my family until I come back for them," I told him, standing to my feet.

"You have my word," he confirmed, reaching his hand out to shake mine. "When you come back, there is something that I want to talk to you about."

"We can talk about it now. I ain't gotta start packing for the next hour or so," I offered.

"No, it can wait. I need you going into whatever it is you need to handle with a clear mind. We will discuss it when you get back."

"Okay, that works," I agreed.

We sat and chopped it up for a little bit longer until he mentioned him having to catch a flight back to Cuba. Taking the stairs two at a time, I took a quick shower and eased in the bed behind Empriss, and cuddled up to her. All I wanted to do was spend the rest of my night with her, stress free and enjoying her company. I didn't know what tomorrow held for me, and I just wanted to cherish everything while it was in front of me. I laid in the dark for a little over an hour, trying to ease my racing mind, until sleep took over my body.

CHAPTER TWENTY-FIVE

Empriss

*H*amin hadn't even been gone for a full hour yet before I swung my legs over the bed and started to get ready for my doctor's appointment. I had a little over an hour to get there, and I still needed to make sure that Lulu was coming to sit with JJ for the weekend while I was gone.

Hamin would kill me if he knew what I was up to, but I just couldn't keep sitting on the information that I had. It was already killing me that I had to wait this long. The plan was to head to my doctor's appointment to check on my newest addition, drive down to Memphis, handle the people that killed Mama Jo, and make it back home to Miami before Hamin even knew that I was gone. Simple. Get there, get back, and act like I had been home all weekend, being the perfect little angel.

The whole time I was getting dressed, I swear my heart was beating out of my chest, and every little noise I heard made me jump, like Hamin would walk in the room any minute, letting me know that I was busted.

"Calm down, Empriss. Hamin is halfway to Memphis right now, and what are the odds that the two of you will even bump into each other?" I said trying to give myself a pep talk.

It took me a little over thirty minutes to handle my hygiene, get dressed and rush out the door to my appointment. I actually was excited about it because it was the last time I would see Harmony's little face before she graced us with her presence, and it gave Hamin a head start to get to where he was going before I got on the road behind him. So, it was a win-win.

Pulling up in front of my doctor's office, I got out of the car and immediately started to take in my surroundings. I suddenly got this weird feeling that someone was watching me. When I didn't see anything out of the ordinary, I chalked it up to me being nervous about Hamin again and shook it off.

The appointment lasted a little more than an hour, and I was overjoyed to hear that my baby girl was right on track. I was thirty-two weeks today and she was already five pounds, so that meant that she was going to be a big baby. If she kept gaining weight and growing on track, she would most likely be a nine-pound baby!

Rushing back home, I ran upstairs and changed out of my clothes into something a little more comfortable. Settling on some black joggers, a black tank top, and some cute black Chanel flats, I was dressed and ready to go. Grabbing my suitcase out of the closet and small duffle, I tried to ease down the stairs without making too much noise.

"Going somewhere, Ms. Reed?" Luke asked from behind me,

scaring the shit out of me.

"Uhh, yeah. I have to go visit Papa," I told him, struggling with the bags.

I couldn't have thought all this through because trying to be the next ninja assassin was not the easiest thing to do when you were pregnant. This shit was a lot harder than I anticipated.

"Does Mr. Shakespeare know that you are flying to Cuba, and alone at that?" he asked, grabbing my bags from me and carrying them.

"Do you work for him or me? And what's with the twenty-one questions?" I asked, annoyed.

"I will take that as a no, and I know for a fact that you're not going to visit Mr. Ortis because he isn't in Cuba at the moment. So, that could only mean that you're headed to one place."

"Damn it, Luke, don't do this shit to me right now."

"Why risk everything to follow another lead that may not pan out, and worst of all it could be a trap."

"I have to. I have to at least try," I told him.

"If you're going then so am I."

"No, Luke. You have to stay here with Lulu and JJ. Someone has to protect them."

"And that is exactly what Carlos will do. If you're hell bent on going, then you definitely will not do so alone. Both Hamin and Javier would kill me if they knew that I let you leave Miami alone and something happened to you and Ms. Harmony. Either I come with you, or we don't go at all. The choice is yours," he told me, stopping in his tracks at the bottom of the staircase.

"Ugh, fine," I huffed.

When we made it outside, Esteban had already pulled the black Lincoln around. Rolling my eyes in to the back of my head, I kept quiet and sat in the back seat to sulk. I would be lying if I said I didn't feel a little more comfortable with them beside me, but at the same time, this was something that I wanted to handle alone; but beggars couldn't be choosy.

Since I couldn't get on a plane due to how far along I was in my pregnancy, we didn't make it to Memphis until one o'clock the next morning. Luke and Esteban kept insisting that we go to the hotel to get some rest before we went on my mission, but I couldn't sleep. I had slept long enough on the car ride down here.

My finger trigger was itching something serious, and I needed to get this over with and out my system so that I could get home to my child. When we pulled up to the house, there were two cars in the driveway and a light on in one of the rooms in the house. At first I thought the person might have had company, but when they didn't leave after a good thirty minutes, I started to think that the car belonged to him. We staked out the front of the house for another hour before my nerves and bladder started to get the best of me. Harmony was inside my stomach using my organs for target practice, and it didn't help that I couldn't keep my leg from bouncing every two seconds.

"Come on, guys. It's either now or never," I told the guys, opening the door and easing out.

Checking the street, I saw that it was quiet and the coast was clear as I made my way across the street, screwing on the silencer to my chrome berretta.

Making our way around to the back door, I stood still to listen out for any noise on the other side of the door. When we didn't hear any, I instructed Esteban to pick the lock. Holding my breath, I waited for an alarm system but when it didn't go off, I breathed a sigh of relief and shook my head.

Fucking amateur, I thought.

"Luke, you come inside and make sure that no one leaves out this door. Esteban, you stay out here and make sure that no one comes inside," I instructed in a whisper.

Nodding their head as confirmation, I slipped my heels off and eased inside the house with Luke behind me. Following the noise, I could hear two people talking but I couldn't make out what they were saying, but the voices sounded familiar. Inching closer, just as I was about to peek around the corner, one of the men stood up and walked out of the room, disappearing around a dark hallway. Waiting thirty more seconds, I took a deep breath before easing in the room and seeing that the man that was left was sitting in a chair looking at something in his hands. My heart was beating erratically to the point I could hear it in my ears. I had never been nervous before a kill, but for some reason I couldn't control my heart rate.

Just as I was about to make my presence known, the guy dropped what he was holding onto the coffee table in front of him and stood to his feet.

"Put your hands above your head and turn around slowly," I

demanded in a shaky voice.

Doing as he was told, he put his hands in the air and started to step from around the chair to face me. When our eyes locked, tears came to my eyes and before I realized what I was doing, I ran full force and jumped in to his arms.

"Jaiyce." I cried in his arms crashing my lips against his…

Hamin

"Man, I'm glad you made time to come see me. I been tryin' to get in touch with you like crazy. I finally found somethin' to get us one step closer to finding this chick, man," Khalid explained while I sat in his living room on the couch.

"Yeah, man, shit just been crazy. I found out my girl was pregnant a few months back and I been tryin' to keep shit on lock in the streets. You know how it is," I told him.

"Damn, that's what's up, man. Congratulations! You know what y'all having yet?"

"Thank you, thank you. We having a little girl," I told him, smiling with pride.

"Awww, hell. Time to bring out the shot guns," he joked.

"Don't I know it." I laughed. "Anyway, you said you found a way to get to this chick. How is that?" I asked.

Feeling my phone vibrate in my pocket, I saw Ace was calling me. Hitting the ignore button, I was about to slide it back in my pocket when a message came through.

Ace: 911! Call me NOW!

"Did you hear me, mane?" Khalid asked me, causing me to look up at him.

"Uh, nah, my bad. Say that again," I apologized.

"I said I found a way to make her come to us."

"And how is that?" I asked.

"Open it," he said, gesturing towards the folder that was setting on the table in front of me.

Picking up the folder, I opened it and the first thing I saw caused my blood to boil. There were pictures of JJ from the time he was a baby up until almost recently.

"Shit's brilliant, right? I ran down his granny a couple months back and she led me right to him. I even found the school the little nigga's registered at and everything. The home address that the bitch put for him was a fake. She's smart, I'll give her that, but she ain't as smart as she thinks she is," he gloated.

The sound of this nigga's voice was doing something to me, and I suddenly felt sick to my stomach. Just as I was about to say something, my phone started buzzing in my pocket immediately. Checking the screen, I saw that it was Ace again.

"My bad, here go my girl calling me right now. Where ya bathroom at?" I asked him, standing to my feet.

"Down the hall to ya right," he instructed, sitting down in the chair and sliding the folder I dropped towards him.

"Aight, good lookin' out."

Speed walking out the room, I pressed the talk button, ready to give Ace the order to come in so we could air this nigga out. This shit already hectic enough when he was gunning for Empriss, but now that he knew about JJ, this was a whole other ball game. This nigga had to go, and I mean like yesterday.

"Yo, Ace," I started as soon as I picked up the phone.

"Aye, Hamin! You gotta get outta there like right now my nigga. He's setting you up. I just saw three people crossin' the street, headed your way wit' guns drawn. I'm headin' down the street right now, my nigga, but you gotta go!" he yelled into the phone.

Hanging up the phone, I pulled my nine off my hip headed back to the living room to air this motherfucker out. This nigga tried to play me like I was a pussy and I was far from it. I was gon' make this nigga regret the day that he ever laid eyes on me. Rounding the corner, my eyes bucked out my head as I watched the nigga I was getting ready to kill kissing my baby mama. Ain't this about a bitch!

TO BE CONTINUED

ACKNOWLEDGMENTS

Here we go again. I can't believe I'm at yet another release. The feeling is so surreal, but I know that there is nothing else I'd rather be doing than this.

Girls. Everything that mommy does, she does it to make you proud and to better your future. I strive to show you that you can be better than your circumstance because I became so much more than anyone thought I would be. Alani, Elizabeth, Amelia and Paisley, just know that you all give me purpose. I love you to the death of me.

Kiara. You already know that you are my biggest supporter and you've shown me time and time again that when it us or the world, you'll choose us every time. You're my sister, but you're also my best friend. My little sister harder than most of you… well you know the rest lol. I love you to the moon and back. We almost there, love. Nowhere to go but up from here.

Sa'ja Jay. Gooonnnnnnnnnnnn! You have been rockin' wit' me since the day we met, and I appreciate that from the bottom of my heart. I say I'm a mini you in so many ways, but you have helped me grow as well as I've helped you. They say get friends that force you to level up, and that's definitely the type of boss move we on. They playin' checkers, while we playin' chess. The world is our playground and I know we about to take the literary world by storm. Love you boo and we only headed up from here.

Shontea'. It's crazy how a friendship developed off you just being a test reader of mine. We clicked immediately and now I can't go a day without you talking some sense into me lol; but no lie, I appreciate you for rocking with me ma, and I'm glad to call you my friend.

To the readers that I gained from *You Give Me Purpose to Love,* I want to thank you from the bottom of my heart for taking a chance on me. Y'all make all of this worthwhile. If you heard about me due to *The Vendetti Family: Money, Murder, Mayhem,* then I thank you as well. And even for the ones that are picking up this one right here, I thank you as well. I hope y'all enjoy this book as much as I enjoyed writing it. I fall in love with all my characters and I hope you will too.

CONNECT WITH ME ON SOCIAL MEDIA TO GET TO KNOW THE WRITER BEHIND THE PEN.

Facebook: Porschea Jade

Twitter: @IAmPorscheaJade

Snapchat: simply_porschea

IG: Simplyy_porscheajade

Periscope: @iamporscheajade

Facebook readers group: Porschea Jade's Urban Exscape

BOOKS BY PORSCHEA JADE:

You Give Me Purpose to Love (standalone)

The Vendetti Family: Money, Murder, & Mayhem

The Vendetti Family 2: Money, Murder & Mayhem (the finale)

The Love a Boss Gives (standalone)

Looking for a publishing home?

Royalty Publishing House, Where the Royals reside, is accepting submissions for writers in the urban fiction genre. If you're interested, submit the first 3-4 chapters with your synopsis to submissions@royaltypublishinghouse.com.

Check out our website for more information: www.royaltypublishinghouse.com.

Text ROYALTY to 42828 to join our mailing list!

To submit a manuscript for our review, email us at
submissions@royaltypublishinghouse.com

Text RPHCHRISTIAN to 22828 for our
CHRISTIAN ROMANCE novels!

Text RPHROMANCE to 22828 for our
INTERRACIAL ROMANCE novels!

Get LiT!

Download the LiT eReader app today and enjoy exclusive content, free books, and more

Do You Like CELEBRITY GOSSIP?

Check Out QUEEN DYNASTY!
Visit Our Site: www.thequeendynasty.com

CPSIA information can be obtained
at www.ICGtesting.com
Printed in the USA
LVOW10s2028030517

533142LV00015B/294/P